Author:
Casey Christofferson

Editor:
Jeff Harkness

Layout:
Suzy Moseby

Art Director:
Casey Christofferson

Front Cover Art:
Brian LeBlanc

Cover Design:
Jim Wampler

Interior Art:
Adrian Landeros

Cartography:
Robert Altbauer

Project Manager:
Casey Christofferson

Pathfinder Conversion:
Michael Mars Russell

Frog God Games is:

Bill Webb, Matt Finch, Zach Glazar, Charles A. Wright, Edwin Nagy, Mike Badolato, and John Barnhouse

Frog God Games

ISBN: 978-1-6656-0009-5
PF PoD

Table of Contents

Background 3

Adventure Summary 3

One Last Thing Map 4

Part 1: Jaego is Dead 5
  Preliminary Investigations 5
  The First Haunting 5
  The Second Haunting 5
  The Third Haunting 5

Part 2: Styx, The Underworld, and the Necropolis of Ankev 6
  Why Adventure in the Necropolis of Ankev? 6
  1. Shore of Lost Souls and the Tributary 7
  2. Bone Gate 7
  3. The Ghoul Canyon 8
  4. Amien's Keep 8
  5. Outer Slums 8
  6. The Bone Mill 8
  7. Leathers of the Flesh 8
  8. Lower Ward 9
  9. Inn of the Moldering Corpse 9
  10. Shadow Gate 9
  11. The Sign of the Grinning Skull 9
  12. Kreal's Bookbinder 10
  13. Middle Ward 10
  14. The Nightmare Consortium: Hauntings for Hire 10
  15. Necromancer's Touch 11
  16. The Temple of Orcus 11
  17. Hennian the Glassblower 11
  18. Mizc Kü Tanük Institute 11
  19. Upper Ward 11
  20. Adroculus' Manor 12
  21. The Ruby Chalice 12
  22. Garrison of the Undying Legion 13
  23. Ruins of Ankev's Palace 13
  24. Quad of the Taharqo 13

25. Mausoleum of Shandar 13
  Shandar's Crypt 14

Where is Jaego? 15
  Interviewing Denizens of the Necropolis 15
    Prisoner of Amien 15
    Held by Adroculus 15
    Prisoner in the Ruby Chalice 15
    In the Shadow Lands 15
    Shandar's Mausoleum 15

Jaego is Found! 15

The Return 15

Further Adventure 15

Appendix A: New Monsters 16
  Acolyte of Orcus 16
  Antipaladin of Orcus 16
  Adroculus the Sacrificer 16
  Bone Gate 17
  Cainor the Skin Stitcher 17
  Ghoul Lord Amien 18
  Hukeesh the Necromancer 18
  Kreal the Bookbinder 19
  Lysipus the Bone Cobbler 20
  Professor Axeworm Armitage III 20
  Ramn Pujab 21
  Rat, Barrow (Ghoulish) 21
  Shandar the Lich Queen 22
  Shandar's Familiar, Rawhide 22
  Sir Ulatuan 23

Appendix B: New Items 24
  Armor of Undeath 24
  Leaden Knot of the Underworld 24
  Vials of Life (Minor Artifact) 24
  Wraith Armor 24

One Last Thing

By Casey Christofferson

A Pathfinder adventure designed for 4 to 6 characters of 7th to 9th level

One Last Thing is an adventure for 4–6 characters of 7th–9th level, though elements of the adventure locations described here may be suitable for much higher-level play.

The adventure begins in a town, city, castle, or somewhere familiar to the characters where they know various NPC friends they have met along the way. The adventure assumes familiarity with a large town or city and nearby graveyard where the Necropolis of Ankev can be accessed.

Background

A friend has passed to the great beyond. Drinks and libations have been had at his wake and a funeral has lain him to his final rest. Something, however, seems hollow and different about the affair. There is unfinished business, and everyone knows it — yet nobody knows just what it is that everyone seems to have forgotten. Days and weeks stretch by, and things seem to remind you of the loss. It feels almost that the dearly departed has some other task, some incomplete goal that must be achieved before it can move on. Something damning has trapped them in the Underworld and only through the deeds of their closest friends may a final and lasting rest be achieved.

One Last Thing is a haunting trek into the Underworld of the freshly dead to find the one last thing that a dead friend needs to rest in peace once and for all. Through the course of the adventure, characters encounter a variety of challenges involving roleplaying, exploration, investigation, and extra-dimensional travel.

Adventure Summary

This adventure requires a little more groundwork to set things up. First off, it requires the characters to know and trust an NPC who is familiar with their career and exploits. For the purposes of the adventure, this NPC is called "Jaego," but you can and should substitute any NPC who fits the needs of the scenario. As the adventure begins, the characters learn that "Jaego" is dead. A short time after his death, Jaego begins haunting the characters. First silently, and then with greater amounts of fear-inducing interactions, Jaego leaves clues behind for the characters to figure out exactly what it is that he wants. As the characters pursue the clues that Jaego leaves behind, they eventually wind up at Jaego's gravesite then travel from there to the very outskirts of the Underworld itself where they are led to the fabled Necropolis of Ankev.

The character must carefully navigate the necropolis lest they wear out their welcome in that deathly realm. After exploring the necropolis, the characters eventually come face to face with their friend and discover what Jaego needs to achieve his final rest.

Who is Jaego?

Establishing Jaego as a friend or ally of the characters is a fairly easy endeavor and could be drawn out over 3–6 gaming sessions. For the purposes of the adventure, Jaego serves as a stand-in murder victim who is familiar to the characters. His body was discovered too late to be raised from the dead, and his finances were such that a purchase of such a *raise dead* or *resurrection* spell was impossible as the grim reaper had already laid claim to his soul. The time is short before his soul is traded to Orcus, as so many unclaimed spirits are. It is well known that once a soul is in the custody of the Demon Lord of the Dead, it is doomed forever as a minion of evil.

In life, Jaego was a young bard who never had a hit until he overheard the characters discuss their exploits in a tavern after one of their first adventures. He penned a song in their honor that became popular locally and brought some fame to the characters. Jaego has casually followed the characters ever since. He has been friendly but kept his distance. The characters know him from the fame he heaped upon their name, and the meals and drinks he has quietly but politely plied them with to get their stories. He could be the guy whom they find trapped in the hobgoblin's cell, or he could happen across the characters near the end of a fight, just in time to offer them a boost of inspiration and a bit of healing. Aside from that, he shouldn't be the star of any show before his death. Instead, Jaego is very much the "Hey, do you all remember that guy that is always hanging out?" sort of fellow. In other words, Jaego is a friendly face in the background whom everyone really liked but that nobody can really claim to have known all that well.

So why is Jaego dead? The characters are not Jaego's only topic of interest. Among other things, Jaego was a spy and one-time herald for the court of Count Mercier of Reme, a noble with connections to one of the royal families. Recently, Jaego came into possession of a diary that had some very significant information relating to the rise and fall of regional powers. Jaego was unsure what to do with the information and wanted to share it with the only heroes he knew. Jaego hid the information but was killed by a faction searching for the diary before he could share its secrets with the characters.

Jaego's spirit now seeks to share the location of his secret diary with the characters so that they may decide what best to do with it. The only way for him to tell the characters where he has hidden the diary is by inviting them to visit his restless spirit in the Necropolis of Ankev on the shores of the River Styx!

One Last Thing
1 square = 100 ft.
1
2
3
4
5
6
7
8
9
10
11
12
13
14
15
16
17
18
19
20
21
22
23
24
25
Etherial Border

Part 1: Jaego is Dead

The adventure begins upon the character's arrival to a familiar settlement such as a town, city, or village that they frequent as a home base or headquarters. They are greeted with news from a familiar barkeep or inn owner that their old friend has been murdered while they were away adventuring. The body was discovered in the basement of an abandoned structure in the foreign quarter, a few blocks from a gambling house he was known to frequent. The victim's body was beyond the help of local clerics and was thus rapidly and summarily buried in a simple plot in the local cemetery due to the onset of putrefaction. Investigators and priests spent some time with the body attempting to use magic and other means to determine the identity of the killer. The constables' report indicated that he had been stabbed multiple times and that his heart had been cut out of his body.

Preliminary Investigations

Characters may speak with local temples or authorities but are given much the same information. It is believed that Jaego went to the gaming house to meet someone and that the person or persons he was intent upon meeting never arrived. He left and was next found several days later, dead and mutilated.

The gaming-house: The Game Master may substitute any gaming house in their campaign world or use one from the Lost Lands such as the famous Fortune's Fool casino in Bard's Gate.

Characters who research deeply into Jaego's past find a lot of dead-ends. A successful DC 25 Knowledge (Nobility) reveals that Jaego was once in the employ of Count Mercier of Reme. Further investigation of Count Mercier reveals that he has direct familial ties to royalty and has a long-standing rivalry with Earl Brodchek.

Additional research discovers that both nobles live some distance from the characters' current location and any attempts to look up their emissaries in the city results only in information related to shipping, trade, and business investments involving other local nobles and merchants.

Note: Gathering this level of information should involve extremely outside chances on the part of the characters, at least initially, and the Game Master may use as much or as little of this information as he or she deems necessary to further characters into their exploration of the Necropolis of Ankev so they may discover what their friend's last wish happens to be!

The First Haunting

The first haunting affects each of the characters individually. They may be walking about town on other business. For example, the rogue may be busy picking pockets or running a scam. The fighting types may be shopping for armor polish or training in a local warriors' gymnasium. The wizard may be at a library in their local guildhall exploring arcane secrets. Each is visited with a vision of Jaego. At first, they catch a glimpse out of the corner of their eye or hear the bars of the song that Jaego penned in their honor. When the characters turn to look more closely, the image appears fleeting or disappears completely. They must make a DC 15 Will saving throw (versus fear) or become unnerved by the sensation and attempt to flee the area.

A short time later, Jaego appears as a full apparition before the character(s). He is either sitting near them, or walks up to them, and attempts to speak, though the words cannot be heard. His body is translucent and leaks ectoplasm from the various stab wounds that took his life. Just as he begins to communicate, he dissolves with an anguished look on his face.

Characters may be confused by what has happened. In his place are a few pieces of parchment that the characters may recognize from Jaego's moleskin notebook. Upon the page are several notes from a funerary dirge. The song is called *"City of the Dead."* The song is a lament describing lost souls trapped on the edge of the River Styx where they wait to be taken to the next stop in the afterlife or where Orcus collects them for unending torment in the eternal Abyss.

Characters who research the song in a temple or bard's academy discover that the *"City of the Dead"* is a reference to the fabled Necropolis of Ankev, a waypoint along the River Styx that was once managed by the fabled arch-lich before he parted ways with Orcus, Demon Lord of the Undead.

The Second Haunting

The characters are frightened by a nightmare. In their vision, they see themselves on the street. Suddenly, masked enemies surround them. They hear their words "It's the end for you ..." but the name is muffled. Their flesh is pierced with knives from multiple directions. Pain wracks their body, and they lie in the gravel of an alleyway gasping and bleeding in the street. One of the crimson-masked figures approaches with a long, thin blade. The character feels a heavy pounding in his or her chest as the figure approaches. Then everything goes red.

When they are aware again, the character notes that Jaego is walking next to them. He is trying to say something, as if imploring them to listen. Finally, Jaego steps in front of them with a concerned look on his gaunt face, his glazed eyes imploring the characters. He points to himself and then at the archway of the city graveyard before he vanishes with an anguished gurgle.

As the characters awake, they are denied any benefit of rest. No spells are refreshed nor are any hit points recovered from their sleep.

As they awaken, they hear notes from the *"City of the Dead"* playing in their ears as if sung by Jaego himself.

"There do I wait in the city of the dead,
Here do they trade for years of my soul,
There do I wait, one last thing to be said,
If only you knew what I know.

There do I wait in the City of the Dead,
Where Ankev did fight for his soul,
There do I wait, one last thing to be said,
Wouldn't you like to know?"

The Third Haunting

For Jaego's third haunting, the characters are suddenly wracked with a vision where a mist rises around them, either in their waking hours or in their dreams. The mist clears slightly, and they find they are walking behind Jaego. He walks until he nears a grave covered in freshly turned earth. He points to the gravestone that bears his name. As he points, the ground opens to reveal a broad, damp staircase leading deep into the earth. The sound of rushing waters can be heard somewhere in the cellar-like dankness below.

The characters awaken in the graveyard, standing in full gear amid the many gravestones before an actual opening in the earth. *Detect magic* or other spells and abilities reveal that the opening in the earth is more than it seems and is indeed a portal to another dimension. Each character finds a leaden amulet in the shape of a knot in their hand.

Should the characters brave it at this time, the portal leads to a staircase of 567 steps that takes them to the **Shore of Lost Souls**.

Leaden Knot of the Underworld

Aura faint abjuration; **CL** 3rd; **Slot** neck; **Price** 1,000 gp; **Weight** —

Leaden knots are sacred amulets woven into the wrappings of mummies to protect their physical flesh as it is projected into the Underworld before crossing on to the proper afterlife. However, a leaden knot of the Underworld is an amulet fused with a mild protective magic that causes lesser undead such as skeletons, zombies, ghouls, and such lesser spirits to look upon an individual wearing such an amulet as simply another of the dead and to generally ignore them. This is not to say that the dead won't attack someone wearing such an amulet, especially if ordered to do so, however unintelligent undead are unlikely to attack a wearer unless provoked.

Leaden knots of the Underworld are typically given as gifts from otherworldly powers to clerics of death cults, necromancers, and other travelers of the Underworld to help them avoid unnecessary entanglements with hostile spirits. The amulet affords no other protections. **Feats** Craft Wondrous Item, *hide from undead*; **Cost** 500 gp

Part 2: Styx, The Underworld, and the Necropolis of Ankev

The Styx is the vast river of the dead that flows through all the realms of the lower planes, offering access to the various layers of Hell and the Demonic abyss. The various tributaries of the river flow through the Iron Pit of Tartarus, and across the punishing vistas of the Plane of Agony.

The planar edge of the Styx is often referred to as the Underworld, and it is a place where spirits with unfinished business, undead beings, and those who resist their final damnable fates wait. It is said that at the center of this shadowy realm lies the ruined palace of Ankev the arch-lich. Once a servant of Orcus himself, Ankev stood vigil over the Gates of the Dead for centuries on behalf of his corpulent overlord. Eventually, the lich transcended Orcus' control.

It is rumored that Orcus used his wand to destroy Ankev for his insolence, although his death didn't erase Ankev's influence from the world. Parts of his ancient cadaver and gilded panoply still turn up in reliquaries held in esteem by modern necromancers. The City of the Dead at the edge of the Styx still bears his name and stands as a testament to his power and his folly.

Why Adventure in the Necropolis of Ankev?

Many of the beings who inhabit the necropolis carry items of great power, knowledge, or lore. Here, too, is the place where those of evil persuasion may beseech the lords of the Underworld for the raising and resurrecting of their fallen heroes before the Gates of the Dead. Most are turned away or join the minions of death who inhabit the necropolis. Some few are granted their request, but at a price.

Planar Features of the Necropolis of Ankev

As an extension of the of the Styx, a vast borderland known by most as the Underworld grants visitors the following bonuses and penalties:

Undead in the necropolis have full hit points per Hit Die.

The DC to resist negative channeled energy within the necropolis gains a +4 sacred bonus and the DC to resist positive energy is reduced by 4. Spell Resistance does not apply to this effect.

The special attacks and abilities of undead gain a +2 sacred bonus to their DC.

Coin of the Realm

In the land of the dead there is little need for mortal coin, with perhaps the exception of vampires who use money to bribe mortals, and mummies who hoard it out of a habit that they had in life. Miserly spirits in life covet treasures in the afterlife though it has no value in the necropolis of Ankev. Instead, the coin of the realm in the Underworld is living life energy. This explains in part its trade for living slaves who are variously sacrificed to Orcus or drained of their life until they join the undead or are consumed utterly by them.

Prices listed for most goods and services are listed in days of life offered by the consumer in exchange for the desired product. For example, a character purchasing a potion or scroll must pay a cost equivalent to its gold piece value in days of his or her mortal life. These days are counted against the maximum age of any character paying the price. If characters spend beyond their years of life and maximum age, they die and are raised as wights.

What the Dead Pay

As the dead have no days of life left to pay to avoid the clutches of the Underworld, they must either find living substitutes to siphon life energy from or they must sacrifice those little pieces that remain of their former life in the form of their living Charisma score. Each point of Charisma sacrificed by the newly dead offers them the opportunity to stay a week longer in the Necropolis before crossing over to the realms of the void to suffer at the hands of Orcus or to be traded to the gods of the other dark realms of the dead. Alternately, they may use their Charisma to haunt someone in the land of the living.

For most of the dead, the choice is simple. They feed off living beings they encounter in the Underworld. Every 10 hit points of damage the dead deal to the living grants them another day of life essence that may be spent in the necropolis before they are forced to move on. The dead who sojourn in the Underworld and reach zero Charisma score become shadows or spectres depending on their level before their death.

The Dead vs. the Undead

The dead are fresh souls who find themselves in the Underworld after having been brought across the Styx by a boatman. Most look roughly as they did in life, though signs of their cause of death are evident. Undead are beings who died a horrible death and were brought back as an undead monster by the supernatural forces of the lords of the dead, such as Orcus, or a monster with the spontaneous generation ability.

Dinner of the Dead

Visitors to the Underworld who make a successful DC 25 Knowledge (Religion) know that any food not brought with the party that is consumed in the land of the dead traps the eater in the realms of the dead forever! It is noted that most visitors must bring their own supply of food or conjure their food through prayer to their deity for manna and fresh water.

There is no save for the curse afflicting those who eat in the land of the dead. The curse may be removed only through the power of a *miracle* or *wish* spell, or by finding other egress through a parallel demi-plane. This plane may be accessed only by entering the realm of Orcus himself! For the dead themselves, the food is a formality; many such as ghouls are filled with insatiable hunger, as vampires are filled with an insatiable thirst for living blood. Neither is satisfied by their meals and continuously crave more, as their tortured and damned souls desire ever to be filled with something that is no longer attainable to them yet is ultimately necessary for their survival!

Vials of Life (Minor Artifact)

These vials are tiny phylacteries that the dead use to store years of life siphoned from the living, or pieces of their eternal soul that they sacrifice for goods and services within the city. The vials each hold one year of life. The vials of life are priceless vessels. Drinking from one of the vessels cures the imbiber for 4d4 + 4 hit points and cures any current non-magical diseases and reduces the physical age of the drinker by 1 year. However, drinking one of the vials while in the Underworld may curse the imbiber to remain as a prisoner of the Underworld forever! Each vial of life beyond the first has its own risks to drinking it. Each consecutive vial requires a DC 15 Fortitude saving throw. If the saving throw fails, the character ages 10 years for each previous vial that has been drunk. If the number of vials exceeds the maximum age for the character's chosen race, he or she dies and rises the following day as a lich shade composed of dust and memory. The DC increases by +1 for every vial imbibed by one of the living beyond the second. **Destruction** A vial of life is destroyed if it is exposed to sunlight.

Living Among the Dead

The majority of dead inhabiting the Necropolis of Ankev are still strongly tied to their spirit in so much as they are not generally considered mindless. With the exception of zombies and skeletons created through sacrifice, these beings still have a dim recollection of their life and repeat the same sorts of activities they participated in while alive. They wander, converse, and occasionally collect things. For the most part, the dead yearn for the end of days where they will be called upon by the Lord of the Living Dead to flood forth from the city, along with their brethren in Orcus' home plane, to awaken the unclaimed dead in the land of the living and once and for all scour the universe of the sorrow that the living existence brings. Until that time, they merely wait.

The more powerful of these dead use the relative peace of the Necropolis of Ankev to maneuver for position in the court of Orcus by working out plans to bring about the end of days as it is given to them in verses and prophecy. Vampires, liches, spectres, ghosts, living necromancers, and others scheme with or against one another for their promised fiefdoms in the land of the living once law and good annihilate one another, leaving the world for the dead to rule.

To gain position and strength in the hierarchy of the dead, all require life essence harvested from unfortunate living creatures who find themselves sold or bartered in the Necropolis of Ankev. The highest prizes are sacrificed before the Gate of Orcus that lies beyond the palace-like Mausoleum of Shandar.

1. Shore of Lost Souls and the Tributary

At the bottom of the 576 steps stands a cave on the edge of a narrow underground stream. At the edge of the stream is a mooring post affixed with a length of chain and an iron bell.

This tributary of the River Styx leads to the Necropolis of Ankev. It is accessible only by those who would have business with the dead. For example, a party of heroes seeking to catch the cohorts of a fallen enemy before they attempt to raise their foe at the Gates of the Dead may claim business in the Necropolis.

When the iron bell is rung, a skiff large enough to ferry the passengers arrives in 1d4 rounds. The boatman is a **charonodaemon** who asks what business the characters have on the Shore of Lost Souls. Individuals seeking knowledge or who are searching for a treasure map, item, or piece of information inside the necropolis may declare this as their reason for seeking Ankev's hidden city. The charonodaemon demands 2 pieces of silver or a magic item of at 2,000 gp value from each of the riders. Once paid, he allows the characters to board his skiff and sets out for the Bone Gate.

Charonodaemon CR 9
XP 6,400
hp 105 (Tome of Horrors Complete, "Daemon, Charonodaemon")

Characters foolish enough to kill the charonodaemon find themselves lost on the River Styx. Who knows what shores of the dead their skiff eventually lands upon?

2. Bone Gate

The Bone Gate stands atop a hill a short distance from the quay where the boatman disembarks passengers. Jagged walls made up of bone and skulls from hundreds of different sentient beings speak in unison, challenging visitors about their purpose in the land of the dead.

Travelers are asked what business they have in the land of the dead. The Bone Gate offers characters a second chance to turn back. If no answer is given, the gate does not open. If a poor answer is given, the visitors are asked to leave. If the visitors attack the gate, they likely destroy it, but find that the planar nexus is then closed to them for 24 hours, denying them entrance to the land of the dead until the gate reforms. If the gate is destroyed, nothing lies beyond it save a simple cave. Entering the cave deposits the visitors back upon the quay. A character making a successful DC 20 Knowledge (Planes) check recognizes the temporary closure of the nexus.

If the gate is destroyed, it becomes a one-way gate that leads out of the demi-plane and directly back to the land of the living rather than a two-way gate leading in and out. Roll for random encounters from the ghoul canyon for the duration that visitors wait for the gate to reform.

Bone Gate   **CR 11**
XP 12,800
hp 142 (Appendix A: New Monsters, "Bone Gate")

3. The Ghoul Canyon

This half-mile-long canyon extends beyond the Bone Gate. It is dotted with crumbling charnel houses and age-worn tombstones shrouded in sickly-looking green vapors that rise from jagged fissures in the ground. Dark figures scurry around the edges of the canyon.

Ghoul Canyon Random Encounters

1d12	Encounter
1	2d8 ghouls
2	1d4 ghasts
3	1d4 + 4 cairn rats
4	1d4 + 2 ghoulish cairn rats
5	1d4 rat swarms
6	Brain rat
7–12	No Encounter

Ghoul (2d8)   **CR 1**
XP 400
hp 20 (Pathfinder Roleplaying Game Bestiary, "Ghoul")

Ghast (1d4)   **CR 2**
XP 600
hp 24 (Pathfinder Roleplaying Game Bestiary, "Ghoul, Ghast")

Cairn Rat (1d4 + 4)   **CR 1/4**
XP 100
hp 5 (Tome of Horrors Complete, "Rat, Barrow")

Ghoulish Cairn Rat (1d4 + 2)   **CR 1**
XP 400
hp 5 (Appendix A: New Monsters, "Rat, Barrow [Ghoulish]")

Rat Swarm (1d4)   **CR 2**
XP 600
hp 16 (Pathfinder Roleplaying Game Bestiary, "Rat Swarm")

Brain Rat   **CR 1/2**
XP 200
hp 5 (Tome of Horrors Complete, "Rat, Brain")

4. Amien's Keep

Amien's Keep stands in the corner of a large stone grotto. More a large three-story mansion than an actual fortified structure, it is surrounded by a wall of polished green marble. The keep of **Ghoul Lord Amien** is located along the eastern expanse of the cavern where he exerts his own form of maddening authority over the denizens of the canyon. Although under the direct authority of Shandar, Amien rules as he sees fit, capturing those unfortunate living entities who do not pay his toll and trading them in the necropolis for things to fulfill his own perverse needs. The keep itself is decrepit and in decay. Each floor has roughly 2d4 usable rooms, and there is a 50% chance per room that the characters encounter **1d6 ghouls**, **1d4 ghasts**, or a structural issue requiring a DC 15 Reflex saving throw to avoid suffering 4d6 points of damage from broken timbers and rubble.

Ghoul (1d6)   **CR 1**
XP 400
hp 20 (Pathfinder Roleplaying Game Bestiary, "Ghoul")

Ghast (1d4)   **CR 2**
XP 600
hp 24 (Pathfinder Roleplaying Game Bestiary, "Ghoul, Ghast")

Ghoul Lord Amien   **CR 11**
XP 12,800
hp 160 (Appendix A: New Monsters, "Ghoul Lord Amien")

Treasure: Amien's treasury includes 3 1,000 gp emeralds, a 1,000 gp opal, 2,500 gp in an iron chest, an oil painting of Amien in life standing amid ghouls worth 12,000 gp, a *potion of bull's strength*, and 6 vials of life, each containing a month of life siphoned off unfortunate travelers caught in the Ghoul Canyon.

Amien charges a year of life to mortal passers-by who cross through his realm into the necropolis itself.

5. Outer Slums

The outermost ring of the necropolis consists of the smashed mausoleums and broken tombs of the lesser dead and those wandering souls who are newly arrived in the city. These new dead often seek sanctuary among those spirits yet to be called to the inner rings of the city — and for good reason. Each spirit knows that the closer one gets to the Mouth of Orcus, the closer they are to losing whatever shred of living memory still resides in their decaying brain.

The Outer Slums are separated from the Lower Ward by a 10-foot-high wall topped with jagged iron spikes.

6. The Bone Mill

Bones picked clean of all flesh are piled from floor to ceiling among the walls of this cursed charnel house. Contingents of mindless zombies on treadmills turn the great millwheel that grinds the bones of dismembered skeletons to dust.

Considered a good shopping place for necromancers seeking a quick complement of skeletons to "bone out" their army, the Bone Yard is also an excellent source of ground bone for use in bone meal or material spell components used in the necromantic arts.

A warehouse in the back contains a plethora of additional bones, though none make up a complete skeleton. They are instead the collected remains of a great number of sentient beasts.

Lysipus the bone cobbler runs the Bone Mill. He keeps an amulet designed to store the life essence of his clients. His bone sells for 1 year of life per wagonload, though he pays half that for fresh bones brought to him in bulk.

Lysipus the Bone Cobbler   **CR 5**
XP 1,600
hp 60 (Appendix A: New Monsters, "Lysipus the Bone Cobbler")

7. Leathers of the Flesh

This slaughterhouse trades evenly with the Bone Yard for any "incomplete" corpses sold to them. Leathers of the Flesh is a squat stone building with a chimney that constantly spouts the foul-smelling odors of the tanners' trade. Within may be heard the moans and whimpers of those resigned to the terror of the last hours of their existence. Leathers of the Flesh is operated by **Cainor the skin stitcher**, a wicked being whose greatest pleasure is peeling his victims and devouring their flesh. Cainor makes exquisite leather armor that is highly sought by those who care not that the skin defending them was once the skin of a living, thinking being. Cainor sells his extra scraps for parchment at the neighboring bookbinder.

Cainor the Skin Stitcher   **CR 5**
XP 1,600
hp 50 (Appendix A: New Monsters, "Cainor the Skin Stitcher")

Armor of Undeath

Aura strong abjuration; **CL** 13th **Weight** 15 lbs.; **Price** 18,910 gp

This *+3 leather armor* is crafted from the flesh of humanoid beings and is as soft and supple as one's own skin. The armor offers a +2 profane bonus to saves versus necromantic spells and an additional +2 profane bonus to saves versus the abilities of undead creatures used against the wearer. The armor is decidedly evil in its very nature, however, and gives a –2 to penalty to Charisma-based reactions from those who recognize the leather's source for what it is.

Feats Craft Magical Arms and Armor, *hide from undead*; **Cost** 9,535 gp

Wraith Armor

Aura moderate conjuration; **CL** 9th **Weight** 15 lbs.; **Price** 10,910 gp

This *+2 leather armor* allows the user to assume the incorporeal form of a wraith for 10 rounds per day. While in wraith form, the character gains a touch attack that deals 1d8 points of negative energy damage and ignores armor worn by the wearer's foe.

Feats Craft Magical Arms and Armor, *plane shift*; **Cost** 5,535 gp

8. Lower Ward

The Lower Ward is separated by a simple, unattended iron gate that marks the boundary of the Outer Slums from the city proper.

The Lower Ward rises along the hill upon which the necropolis sits. Made up mostly of row after row of gravestones, single-occupant mausoleums, and aboveground sarcophagi, the Lower Ward's population is mostly skeletons, zombies, and other lesser undead. While these beings are considered mindless in the land of the living, in Ankev's realm they possess a slightly more rudimentary intelligence, though their conversations and aims are akin to those of living commoners. They typically go about their business, paying no mind to living visitors unless bothered or if they believe they are strong enough to dine on the flesh of the living. Well-armed visitors, those displaying holy symbols, or those doused in holy water are left alone unless ordered to act by a more-powerful being. Thousands of skeletons, zombies, and other lost souls wander the Lower Ward or simply rest within a mausoleum or disturbed grave.

9. Inn of the Moldering Corpse

A decrepit brick pile hung with the sign of a rotting corpse sits on a desolate street in the suburbs, butting up against the walls of Ankev proper.

This inn and tavern serves as a waystation for those seeking entry to the necropolis. Within its walls are a variety of visitors from other times and planes of existence, all with some business within the gated city. A variety of services are offered, including rooms and "food" of sorts, though it is the food of the dead and offers its own unique risks for the unwary traveler.

The Inn of the Moldering Corpse is operated by **Grall Tabrel**, a ghost who has seemingly always run the inn. Grall has a gravelly voiced but is polite to visitors who do not attempt to cause problems with him or his establishment. Grall is a fairly good source of information about living visitors and the newly dead since he doesn't care about their plots, concerns, or worries. His freedom with information often proves to be a two-edged sword for those seeking more discreet lodgings, though he may be bribed for the equivalent of one day of life per day of stay in his inn to "keep quiet." Since no other lodgings are in the suburbs, and camping in the Ghoul Canyon brings near-constant attacks, most visitors resign themselves to paying Grall's prices.

Services

Room for the Night	1 day of life essence
Pickled Halfling Brains	2 days life essence
Raw Humanoid	1 day of life essence
Bonemeal Bread	1 day of life essence per loaf, grants +1 profane bonus to saves versus necromantic spells.
Living Blood Slave (not to be drained to death!)	2 years of life essence or 200 gp in magic items. (Typically reserved for vampires or others who feast on blood.)

Renting a room at the Inn of the Moldering Corpse guarantees that the renter is left unmolested by any of the other denizens of the demi-plane, unless the PCs happen to be wanted for high crimes in the necropolis itself. It does not, however, offer protection against other visitors, so let the renter beware!

Grall Tabrel　　　CR 7
XP 3,200
hp 106 (Pathfinder Roleplaying Game Bestiary, "Ghost")

Current Visitors

The following characters are currently holed up at the Inn of the Moldering Corpse:

Sir Ulatuan and the Wights:
Sir Ulatuan is an antipaladin of Orcus who keeps the company of a gathering of 6 wights. Lord Ulatuan goes forth and spreads the gospel of the Lord of the Dead in hopes of achieving the grace of becoming a death knight upon his dying breath. Ulatuan is currently working as a bounty hunter of sorts, collecting lost souls from the shores of the Styx or the Valley of Ghouls and delivering them to the Temple of Orcus.

Sir Ulatuan　　　CR 8
XP 4,800
hp 77 (Appendix A: New Monsters, "Sir Ulatuan")

Wight (6)　　　CR 3
XP 800
hp 40 (Pathfinder Roleplaying Game Bestiary, "Wight")

Lord Ulatuan may be hired to track down Jaego's whereabouts. He charges five years of life for the task, and characters must provide their own vials of life to seal the bargain. Ulatuan finds Jaego's location in 1d4 days but has a 50% chance of cutting a deal with Shandar to deliver the characters to the lich queen.

Hukeesh the Necromancer:
Hukeesh seeks entry to Mïzć Kü Tanük but has yet to collect the amount of life required to barter entrance without succumbing to the touch of death himself. Hukeesh may offer his services as a guide in the Necropolis of Ankev for a year's worth of life essence. He claims deep knowledge of the newly dead and could lead characters to the soul they seek. Hukeesh would trade the information for either admission to Mïzć Kü Tanük or free access to five necromancy spells of 2nd–4th level.

Hukeesh the Necromancer　　　CR 5
XP 1,600
hp 29 (Appendix A: New Monsters, "Hukeesh the Necromancer")

10. Shadow Gate

This planar gate offers passage from the Underworld to the Plane of Shadow, a plane marked by its ghostly resemblance to the world of the living. The gates are guarded by a contingent of **shadows** who deny entrance to the realm of the Shadow Lords. The living must bring one of the dead to act as a spirit guide with them to pass into the realm of shadow. Or they must be willing to sacrifice a portion of their life essence (in the form of strength) to enter the darkness. Those submitting to the touch of the shadows suffer 1 point of strength damage before they are allowed to pass into the plane beyond.

Shadows (2d8)　　　CR 3
XP 800
hp 30 (Pathfinder Roleplaying Game Bestiary, "Shadow")

11. The Sign of the Grinning Skull

This boardinghouse caters to the warrior caste, where skeletal warriors rub elbows with bloody bones as they drink their mugs of dust and revel in tales of how they came to be. The grinning skull is the place to go for an aspiring necromancer looking to recruit unholy warriors of the undead to serve as officers in their armies.

The Sign of the Grinning Skull is run by **Malago**, a **skeletal warrior** who dutifully connects patrons with undead mercenary leaders and their cohorts. Each mercenary commands a squad of 4d8 skeletons or zombies, or 2d8 ghouls.

Rooms can be rented in this dusty mausoleum as well for 2 days of life essence per day of lodging. The renter is protected from assault by other patrons so long as he obeys the house rules and causes no trouble with the other guests.

Malago the Skeleton Warrior　　　CR 2
XP 600
hp 29 (Pathfinder Roleplaying Game Bestiary, "Skeleton, Skeletal Champion")

Add Gear +1 greatsword, +1 full plate armor; **Remove Gear** breastplate, heavy steel shield, masterwork longsword

Hiring the Undead

The following are some examples of undead found in the Sign of the Grinning Skull and the cost in life essence to hire them.

Undead	Cost to Hire
1d4 Black Skeleton Officers	1 year of life each for one year of service
2d4 Juju Zombies	1 year of life each for one year of service.
Barrow Wight	1 year of life for 3 months of service

12. Kreal's Bookbinder

Kreal is a renowned bookbinder who sells blank scrolls and magic books crafted of dwarf, elf, human, dragon, and other various rare skins. Such skins are much sought after by demonologists, necromancers, and other magic-users of the darker arts. A trio of deft goblins assists him in crafting his handmade books. The goblins were long ago fed the food of the dead and can no longer leave the Necropolis of Ankev.

Kreal sells materials used in the crafting of magical books and scrolls.

Kreal the Bookbinder　　　**CR 8**
XP 4,800
hp 41 (Appendix A: New Monsters, "Kreal the Bookbinder")

Items for Sale

Item	Cost in Life Essence
Ink	100 days of life per bottle
Human skin	25 days of life per page
Elf skin	75 days of life per page (+1 caster level when spell is cast from scroll)
Dragon skin	200 days of life per page (+2 caster level when spell is cast from scroll)
Demon, devil, or angel skin	500 days of life per page (+3 caster level when spell is cast from scroll)

13. Middle Ward

Larger numbers of the living dwell in the Middle Ward than the Upper and Lower Wards, as it is the location of the Temple of Orcus, The Nightmare Consortium, and the fabled Mïzć Kü Tanük University and its fabled library. Aside from the campus and the apartments of Orcus' acolytes, and the crypts of the university faculty, a few other shops or amenities are found here for those beings not interested in the affairs of Orcus' living worshippers.

14. The Nightmare Consortium: Hauntings for Hire

The Nightmare Consortium is a loose coalition of spirits who hire themselves out to perform haunting activities in the land of the living. Typically, necromancers or evil warlords seek them to serve as guardians of their keeps. Wicked nobles also use them to haunt the homes of their political rivals.

Their typical term of service is one year for each living soul traded, or one week for each day of life traded. As usual, the most common form of payment is in prisoners traded to the consortium, who in turn trade the unfortunate prisoners at the Temple of Orcus, thus furthering their own goal in achieving their paradise in the realm of Orcus.

The nightmare consortium houses a variety of phantoms, spectres, wraiths, poltergeists, and ghosts, all with a particular penchant for the horrific. Business with the consortium is managed by **Ramn Pujab** an Illusionist with some training in the necromantic arts. Ramn interviews potential customers, fixing them up with the particular spirit of their needs. Once the needs of the customer are established, they are given a soul jar housing the undead intended to fulfill their purpose.

Ramn Pujab　　　**CR 9**
XP 6,400
hp 45 (Appendix A: New Monsters, "Ramn Pujab")

At any given time, 1d4 of the following spirits are on the premises of the Nightmare Consortium. Hiring them costs life essence.

Undead	Cost in Life Essence
Ghosts	1 year of life per month of service
Wraiths	1 year of life per 3 months of service
Spectres	1 year of life per 6 months of service

15. Necromancer's Touch

The necromancer's touch is managed by Zara Darksilk, a drider who weaves most of the clothes herself.

The shop features fashions and accessories for the discerning necromancer. Robes, capes, turbans, caps, black lipstick, and lace gloves can all be found here to help the living add that fresh "touch of death" to their ensemble.

Zara Darksilk   CR 7
XP 3,200
hp 76 (Pathfinder Roleplaying Game Bestiary, "Drider")

Sample Items

Item	Cost in Life Essence
Velvet cowl	50 days of life
Lace gloves	50 days of life
Red and black velvet mantlet embroidered with rubies	2,000 days of life (affords a +1 armor bonus to armor class, 0% spell failure, -0 ACP, weighs 1 lb.)
Black velvet robes	100 days of life
Drider silk pantaloons	250 days of life
Diamond crusted eyepatch	500 days of life
Thigh-high leather boots (red or black)	200 days of life

16. The Temple of Orcus

This open-air temple is carved in the shape of a pair of clawed skeletal hands and a grinning skull. A bowl held between the hands turns any corpse thrown into it into a zombie, skeleton, or other undead based on the victim's hit dice. **Adroculus the Sacrificer** oversees the temple's day-to-day activities. He is assisted by a pair of acolytes and guarded by a squad of guardsmen from the Undying Legion that he commands utterly. Adroculus keeps an apartment in a mansion-sized mausoleum not far from the temple and awaits the day when his god calls him to join the undead as one of their own.

Typically, a line of 2d12 chained slaves awaits sacrifice upon the steps leading to the bowl. Among these are an additional 2d20 lost dead who have run out of Charisma, vials of life, or hope — or all three — and find their spirit forms further mutilated during the sacrifice.

The altar at the top of the steps is where Adroculus cuts out the hearts of the wretched victims, casting them to the milling crowd of zombies, ghouls, and vampire spawn who often wrestle for their morsels. Upon completing the sacrifice, Adroculus reawakens the dead as zombies, skeletons, or some greater undead with an enchanted staff given him by Shandar. The horrid sacrifices end when the charges of the staff are expended, and due to the magic of this temple recharges completely while inside it.

The bowl of the temple is an open one-way portal leading to layers of the Abyss ruled by Orcus. Spirits unclaimed by other gods that are cast through the portal soon find themselves turned into dretches, quasits, or larvae of the lower planes.

Adroculus the Sacrificer   CR 11
XP 12,800
hp 67 (Appendix A: New Monsters, "Adroculus the Sacrificer")

Typically, those who come to the Necropolis of Ankev to raise their dead allies are turned away by Orcus. In this event, they are directed to find Adroculus, who offers transformation to undeath instead. His price to perform the ritual is 999 days of life or a living sacrifice of a sentient being to Orcus.

17. Hennian the Glassblower

Hennian crafts vials of life from sand collected from the shores of the River Styx. Empty vials of life cost a year of life to purchase but may be used to absorb life from those willing to give up their years to fill these curious bottles.

Hennian the Glassblower CR 13
XP 25,600
hp 171 (Tome of Horrors Complete, "Hag, Pit")

Treasure: Hennian has 4 vials of life with a year of life in each, a *cloak of elvenkind*, a *ring of jumping*, 1,800 gp, and a ruby ring worth 350 gp.

18. Mïzć Kü Tanük Institute

Mïzć Kü Tanük Institute is a secretive and highly sought institute for study of necromancy and the occult. Necromancers from various planes often seek the Necropolis of Ankev merely to attend courses of study or to purchase spells from the fabled library.

Lectures are given on occasion by liches and other masters of the undead, including such foul luminaries as Jhedophar, Athransma, and Earl Damien Aerim.

Admittance to the institute requires a year of life. Any spells or knowledge to manufacture magic items requires additional payment, either in months, sacrifices, or trade in magical items.

New necromancer spells may be scribed into spellbooks for the cost of one month of life per level of the spell. Thus, a 1st-level spell requires sacrificing one month of life, while a 9th-level spell requires 9 months of life.

The institute is the only place in the Necropolis of Ankev where leaden knots can be purchased. The amulets cost 1 year of life each.

The institute is administered by the ghost of **Professor Axeworm Armitage III**. Axeworm served as a living sage when the institute was founded and has remained at his post for nearly 400 years.

He is assisted by **12 wraiths** who ensure that the books are not harmed and that visiting students respect the sanctity of the institution.

Professor Axeworm Armitage III   CR 9
XP 6,400
hp 97 (Appendix A: New Monsters, "Professor Axeworm Armitage III")

Wraith (12)   CR 5
XP 1,600
hp 65 (Pathfinder Roleplaying Game Bestiary, "Wraith")

Axeworm is privy to a great deal of information about the comings and goings of spirits and the political winds of the necropolis. For five years of life, he shares the location of Jaego should the characters ask.

The corpses of the wraiths are buried in the faculty crypts on the campus grounds. Their tombs contain a variety of treasures that they held dear in life. However, searching the crypts without first dealing with the wraiths could prove problematic as the wraiths appear in 1d4 rounds to defend their worldly treasures.

Treasure: 4 vials of life worth 1 year of life each, a *mariner's eye patch*, *gloves of restrained death*, a *staff of electricity*, *cloak of the hedge wizard (abjuration)*, 24 sp, and a *gem of seeing*.

19. Upper Ward

The tombs, crypts, and mausoleums of the upper ward are much larger and of higher quality though smaller in number than those found in the Middle and Lower wards. Elite visitors are guided to the Ruby Chalice for shows and events or sent to the Bloodless Court to seek lodging more discerning and sublime than those found in the Lower Ward or the suburban outskirts of the necropolis.

20. Adroculus' Manor

This manor house serves as the home of Adroculus the High Priest of Orcus. The multiroom structure is tended by **4 lesser priests of Orcus** and is guarded by a force of **10 antipaladins** in service of the lord of the dead.

The doors to Adroculus' private chambers are cursed. The curse (DC 21) causes its victims to fail any save versus the special powers of an undead creature.

Within his chambers are a locked bronze-bound chest trapped with contact poison smeared on the lock that causes its victim to collapse in a near-death state for 2d6 hours. The poison is nearly undetectable by non-magical means. The poison is Tears of Death. The poison requires a DC 30 Perception check to detect and avoid. The lock requires a DC 20 Disable Device check to unlock. The chest contains the following treasures.

Tears of Death

Type poison (contact); **Save** Fortitude DC 22; **Onset** 1 minute;
  Frequency 1/minute for 6 minutes; **Cure** —
Effect 1d6 Con damage and paralyzed for 1 minute

Treasure: 10 vials each containing a year of life.

Acolyte of Orcus (4) CR 3
XP 800
hp 22 (Appendix A: New Monsters, "Acolyte of Orcus")

Antipaladin of Orcus (10) CR 3
XP 800
hp 30 (Appendix A: New Monsters, "Antipaladin of Orcus")

21. The Ruby Chalice

The Ruby Chalice is a vampire-run cabaret catering to upscale clientele and intelligent undead who still have a bit of zeal and zest for life, particularly for the life essence and blood of the living!

Romeo Nacht, an agent of the Underguild, is the proprietor of the Ruby Chalice. He is assisted by **6 vampiric spawn**. Romeo has allies among many slaving organizations on a dozen different planes who fill his quota of fresh hot blood and timid, sorrowful souls to appease the tastes of his clientele. One such organization with which Romeo is connected is the Underguild and their infamous chain of taverns and bordellos.

The cabaret features entertainment twice daily in the form of skits, dance ensembles, and dirges performed by bands of the living and the dead. One of the more popular shows is a comedy performance put on by **Zuriel Von Dokker**, the wraith of a wizard left unburied by his fellow adventurers after they plundered his corpse for the gear and loot he carried.

Equally popular are the Juliettes, Romeo's dancing girls, who do a cancan dance. These comely vampire spawn each fell in love with Romeo in life, were willingly turned, and are now loyal to him above all else. The dancers are known to charm living visitors to the Ruby Chalice into sacrificing their blood and life essence.

Unlike most other locales within the Necropolis of Ankev, Romeo is still very much addicted to the trappings of life, especially magic items, and often takes payment in magic or living slaves in lieu of the years of life that other denizens accept.

Wares: Aside from lively entertainment, the following succulent items may be selected off the Ruby Chalice's menu.

Romeo Nacht CR 9
XP 6,400
hp 120 (Pathfinder Roleplaying Game Bestiary, "Vampire")

Add Gear *+1 rapier*

The Juliettes (6) CR 4
XP 1,200
hp 40 (Pathfinder Roleplaying Game Bestiary, "Vampire Spawn")

Zuriel Von Dokker CR 5
XP 1,600
hp 65 (Pathfinder Roleplaying Game Bestiary, "Wraith")

Menu Items

Eating the food at the Ruby Chalice comes with specific risks and rewards. The deleterious effects of the food served may be cured with a *remove curse* or *restoration* spell.

Living Blood Slave (not to be drained to death!)	2 years of life essence or 200 gp in magic items per draught. (Typically reserved for vampires or others who feast on blood.)
Nether Ambrosia	There is nothing so sweet as the food of the gods. Sweeter still is the food of the dead. Mortals consuming the nether ambrosia must make a successful DC 15 Fortitude saving throw or be struck dead by the rush of flavors. Those who die rise as wights within 24 hours.
Midnight Wine	The wine of the underworld, midnight wine forces deep and troubled dreams upon the living. The dreams are sometimes portentous, but as often as not lead to a long coma and slow death. Imbibers must make a successful DC 16 Fortitude saving throw or fall into a coma lasting 1d4 days. At the end of each day, the drinker must make another saving throw. If this fails, the drinker dies and rises as a wraith upon the start of the next evening. Drinkers who succeed on their saving throw are faced with visions that award them knowledge of their next dangerous encounter, the solution to an upcoming puzzle or trap, or a free reroll of their choice.
Grave Truffles	Also called coffin fruit, this fungus grows upon old, decaying coffins. The grave truffle is a true delicacy to the dead. Those who can withstand the initial bite of the grave truffle gain an increased fortitude against the effects of the dead. Eaters must make a successful DC 15 Fortitude saving throw after ingesting grave truffles. Failure causes 4d6 points of negative energy damage. On a successful save, the eater gains a +2 profane bonus to saves versus the effects of undead such as ghoulish paralysis or mummy rot for 24 hours.
Death by Chocolate	This desert is favored by fiends of Hell and the Abyss for its pure decadence. When eaten by mortals, this chocolate cake, pudding, and liquor syrup delicacy fills them with euphoria and a sense of satisfaction and vigor unlike anything else they have ever experienced. Eating a treat meant for the damned, however, comes at a cost. As the flavor of death by chocolate is so intense, no other food may ever sate their hunger again. Mortals must make a successful DC 17 Fortitude saving throw or waste away, suffering 1d4 points of Constitution drain per day as they uncontrollably shed weight until they eventually die from starvation. On a successful save, the character gains a temporary profane bonus of +2 to their Constitution and Charisma scores that lasts for 24 hours.

22. Garrison of the Undying Legion

This barracks houses **30 fear guards** led by **Lord Kartillion the Heathen**, a **death knight** who rides a stout **nightmare**.

Once a paladin of law and justice, Lord Kartillion was driven mad during a long-forgotten crusade during which he was given orders to sack cities that had surrendered and to put prisoners to the sword. After murdering his fellow generals and his crown prince in a fit of rage, Kartillion swore allegiance to the banner Orcus, Lord of the Dead, before leading his men on a rampaging crusade of bloodlust and murder across three kingdoms of Libynos. Kartillion and his core of 30 battle-mad knights met their end at the end of the lances of the Numedan cavalry nearly 500 years ago.

In death, Kartillion has crawled his way from the pits of the Abyss and now commands the damned souls of his old brigade once more in the form of Shandar's own private police force.

Fear Guard (30)   CR 5
XP 1,600
hp 72 (Tome of Horrors Complete, "Fear Guard")

Lord Kartillion the Heathen CR 10
XP 12,800
hp 135 (Tome of Horrors 4, "Death Knight")

Nightmare   CR 5
XP 1,600
hp 51 (Pathfinder Roleplaying Game Bestiary, "Nightmare")

23. Ruins of Ankev's Palace

A field of rubble is all that remains of the once-mighty palace of Ankev, former chosen herald of Orcus. The field retains naught but broken stone since the destruction of Ankev's palace and the rending of his form across the cosmos.

24. Quad of the Taharqo

These 400-foot-tall pyramids form a quad to the south of the Mausoleum of Shandar and serve as the resting place of **Peimeroe Taharqo** and his **3 mummy sons**. These famed warrior princes of ancient Khemit now hold spectral court here for all eternity.

Taharqo and his sons seldom venture from their tombs, but when they do, it is in force, with the four of them fighting in unison as they did when they established the southern dynastic line. The four are able to open a gate to the Astral Plane where Ammit and Anubis wait to judge the heart and soul of those who become lost on their way to the afterlife.

Taharqo opens the gate to the Scales of Judgement for 10 years of life or 10 points of Charisma.

Peimeroe Taharqo, Crown Prince CR 10
XP 9,600
hp 155 (Pathfinder Roleplaying Game Bestiary 5, "Mummy Lord")

Remove Gear *+1 spear, scroll of spiritual weapon, scroll of summon monster III* **Add Gear** *+1 heavy mace, brass horn of valhalla*

Sons of Taharqo (3)   CR 5
XP 1,600
hp 88 (Pathfinder Roleplaying Game Bestiary, "Mummy")

Treasure: *Potion of bull's strength, marvelous pigments, scroll of plane shift, scroll of contingency,* 18,000 gp, *robe of the archmagi (black),* and 20 vials of life containing 1 year of life each.

25. Mausoleum of Shandar

As Ankev fell, so did Shandar rise from his ashes. A faithful sorceress steeped in the necromantic arts, Shandar performed the rites and rituals of eternal undeath as soon as the first touches of age began to stretch their skein across her brow. Shandar had studied at the foot of many of the moldering lich lords, absorbing their magic and studying the craft of their phylacteries. She drank deeply of the living souls bartered in the necropolis at the edge of the Abyss to extend her own age unnaturally.

For a living corpse, Shandar almost appears to be a freshly fed vampire, save for a waxy sheen and the thick stench of formaldehyde she exudes like a sickly perfume. Shandar lazily observes the happenings within the necropolis from within the depths of her labyrinthine tomb.

The mausoleum's maze is said to be controlled by the Shandar's own thoughts, requiring a genius to navigate the twisting passageways without becoming completely lost. Aside from the ever-changing maze, the mausoleum is also filled with traps that are mechanical and magical in nature.

Characters must make five successful DC 20 Intelligence checks to find their way through the maze. On a failed check, the characters become lost and encounter a trap. Suggested traps are listed below. After five successful checks, the characters find themselves in Shandar's crypt.

1   **Smashing Wall Trap:** This trap is triggered by the third figure to step onto a hidden plate. The trap may be disarmed by wedging the plate so that it cannot depress.

Smashing Wall Trap   CR 6
XP 2400
Type mechanical; **Perception** DC 14; **Disable Device** DC 16
Trigger location; **Reset** none
Effect Atk +20 melee (8d6, stone blocks); multiple targets (all targets within 10 ft.)

2   **Lighting Field Trap:** This trap is set off by a change in electromagnetic energy brought about by living beings passing through the field. The floor and walls of this area are lined with copper inlay that spell out the words "Goodbye, Thieves," in the elvish, dwarvish, gnomish, common, and abyssal tongues. Noticing the writing requires a successful DC 20 Perception check. Characters can disable the trap by rubbing wool on the word "good" in the abyssal script to neutralize the field's polarity.

Lightning Field Trap   CR 6
XP 2,400
Type magical; **Perception** DC 28; **Disable Device** DC 28
Trigger proximity (passing through the field); **Reset** no
Effect spell effect (three *lightning bolts* one after another in the same round, 6d6 damage each, Reflex DC 15 half each)

3   **Pit Trap:** This pit is well hidden. A character may spike the lid, preventing it from tipping and dropping the characters 50 feet into a 5-foot-by-5-foot cube of **green slime**. The sides of the wall are covered in a slick greasy substance that make it a challenge to climb out of the pit, requiring a DC 20 Climb check.

Slimy Pit Trap   CR 3
XP 800
Type mechanical; **Perception** DC 20; **Disable Device** DC 20
Trigger location; **Reset** manual
Effect 50-ft.-deep pit (5d6 falling damage plus green slime); DC 20 Reflex avoids; multiple targets (all targets in a 10-ft.-square area)

Green Slime   CR 4
XP 1,200
This dungeon peril is a dangerous variety of normal slime. Green slime devours flesh and organic materials on contact and is even capable of dissolving metal. Bright green, wet, and sticky, it clings to walls, floors, and ceilings in patches, reproducing as it consumes organic matter. It drops from walls and ceilings when it detects movement (and possible food) below.
A single 5-foot square of green slime deals 1d6 points of Constitution damage per round while it devours flesh. On the first round of contact, the slime can be scraped off a creature (destroying the scraping device), but after that it must be frozen, burned, or cut away (dealing damage to the victim as well). Anything that deals cold or fire damage, sunlight, or a *remove disease* spell destroys a patch of green slime. Against wood or metal, green slime deals 2d6 points of damage per round, ignoring metal's hardness but not that of wood. It does not harm stone.

4   **Hall of Spears Trap:** Phalanxes of spears are hidden in the walls of this 30-foot-long hallway. These spears come from the floor, ceiling, or walls. They are cleverly hidden in carvings featuring the grandeur of Shandar's rise to power. The phalanxes can be disabled with a hidden lever buried inside a carved skull at the outset of each end of the hallway.

Hall of Spears Trap CR 3
XP 800
Type mechanical; **Perception** DC 20; **Disable Device** DC 20
Trigger location; **Reset** automatic (triggers every round)
Effect Atk spear +10 melee (1d8/x3); multiple targets (everyone in the hall)

5   **Wall of Ice Trap:** Bearing a torch through this section of the corridor causes walls of ice to spring up 10 feet in front and behind the party. The ice quickly flows across the floor and ceiling around them, thus narrowing the tunnel and effectively trapping them within a 10-foot-by-20-foot ice cube.

Wall of Ice Trap   CR 10
XP 9,600
Type magic; **Perception** DC 30; **Disable Device** DC 30
Trigger proximity (alarm); **Duration** 12 minutes; **Reset** automatic
Effect spell effect (wall of ice surrounds 10-foot-by-20-foot cube; CL 12th); extreme cold (1d6 cold damage/minute; creatures in contact with exposed metal take an additional 1d6 points of cold damage per round); multiple targets (all creatures in the cube)

6   **Monster Summoning:** Characters notice a rune of cold and a rune of summoning on the floor and ceiling of the hallway they are about to enter with a successful DC 30 Perception check. The trap may be disabled with *dispel magic* or a DC 30 Disable Device check. Crossing into the area without noticing the rune triggers the trap, which calls a large **silver bulette** that attacks immediately.

Bulette   CR 7
XP 3,200
hp 84 (Pathfinder Roleplaying Game Bestiary, "Bulette")

SHANDAR'S CRYPT

Shandar the lich queen resides within her large stone crypt, spending her hours observing the goings-on of the city with her *crystal ball with detect thoughts* and preparing herself for the inevitable decay of her flesh. The crypt walls are hung with black velvet. Under the velvet are a dozen silver mirrors where the once beautiful but now waxen queen of the Necropolis of Ankev once observed her comely form.

Shandar leaves the confines of her crypt only when meting out punishment within the necropolis. Such events tend to be few and far between, though it is not unusual for her to send her cacodaemon **Rawhide** out to the city to collect a misplaced soul for her amusement.

Shandar the Lich Queen   CR 12
XP 19,200
hp 132 (Appendix A: New Monsters, "Shandar the Lich Queen")

Rawhide   CR –
XP –
hp 66 (Appendix A: New Monsters, "Shandar's Familiar, Rawhide")

Treasure: Shandar's treasury is hidden within a portable hole found folded into a book upon the bookshelf standing next to her crypt. Within the portable hole are 3,300 gp, 1,000 platinum, 3 sapphires worth 1,000 gp each, 1 diamond worth 2,000 gp, a fire opal worth 1,000 gp, a map of the City of Brass with the address of Rah'po Dehj marked on it, a potion of cure serious wounds, a scroll of plane shift, a potion of haste, and 10 vials of life each containing 1 year of life each.

Where is Jaego?

It is left up to the Game Master where to place Jaego, but listed below are locations and reasons why he might be trapped there. Characters will need to use their role-playing skills to locate Jaego, and access to his spirit may be contingent on completing a quest for the being currently holding his spirit hostage. Listed below are possible places where Jaego's captured spirit may be located.

Interviewing Denizens of the Necropolis

Characters may talk to the random dead they encounter in the Necropolis of Ankev to determine the whereabouts of Jaego's spirit. Talking to a random intelligent undead off the street has a 1-in-20 chance of giving them a clue to his whereabouts.

Talking to proprietors of one of the city's shops or taverns offers a 5-in-20 chance of receiving useful information about Jaego's current location.

Hiring Lord Ulatuan or Hukeesh guarantees Jaego's location is revealed but comes with its own dangers. Alternately, the characters may visit the institute to ask Axeworm if he knows anything.

Prisoner of Amien

Amien noticed that the newly dead Jaego was taking great efforts to contact the living, especially for one who had been in the Underworld for such a short period of time. Amien captured Jaego's Underworld form and now holds it in his manor house.

Amien demands that the characters bring him a willing sacrifice to Orcus. Either that, or he requires 20 filled vials of life in exchange for their friend's restless spirit.

Held by Adroculus

Adroculus is aware that Jaego reached beyond the land of the dead for some form of aid. If approached, Adroculus offers to trade Jaego's spirit for one of the living characters, whom he then intends to sacrifice to Orcus.

Prisoner in the Ruby Chalice

Romeo Nacht is holding the spirit of Jaego. He is willing to trade Jaego's spirit if someone agrees to serve him for a year as his willing blood slave. He'll also accept a powerful magic item of the GM's choice.

In the Shadow Lands

Jaego's spirit hid on the Plane of Shadow, but was captured by the Shadow Demon Shoren and is currently being held in the city of Dehenet (detailed in *The Sword of Air* by **Frog God Games**).

Shandar's Mausoleum

Jaego is currently a prisoner in Shandar's Mausoleum. Shandar demands that the characters go forth and recover one of the Letek're stones from the Isle of Eliphaz (detailed in Isle of Eliphaz in Quests of Doom Volume 2 from Frog God Games).

Remember that the above are simply suggestions. A creative GM may have a better location or may use a plot hook more appropriate to his or her campaign world.

Jaego is Found!

Jaego's spirit is weak and much diminished due to his great expenditure of Charisma to make contact with the characters from the Underworld. Once Jaego is recovered, he tells them the story of a secret diary he hid behind some bricks in the booth of his favorite tavern. Jaego thanks them for being such good friends to him in life, and for serving as an inspiration to his art. He explains that the diary contains damning information about the true parentage of an heir to a pair of noble houses and leaves it to the characters to decide what is best to do with the diary and the information contained therein. He feels responsible for the contents of the diary but believes the characters will know best what to do and has resigned himself to joining the damned either in the Abyss or the Hells. After revealing his truth and the secret location of the diary, Jaego thanks them again for what they have done for him both in life and in death. With that, his spirit seemingly fades away.

The Return

Characters may return to the surface world by summoning a boatman and paying him his fee of two silvers each.

Choices

The ledger reveals that Jaego is the true father of Lord Mercier and Earl Brodchek's grandson. The Council of Reme ordered Mercier's daughter to marry Earl Brodchek's son as a means of creating peace between the warring families. The Brodchek family suspected something was amiss when the child was born eight months after the wedding. The child was small at birth, and the wetnurses explained that the child was simply born too early. Brodchek was still not convinced and received word that the Mercier's longtime herald had left the count's banner. He dispatched his agents to track down Jaego for questioning. The search took years because Jaego had done a good job of covering his tracks — until recently.

In the meantime, the marriage between the Mercier and Brodchek family resulted in a truce of sorts as the business and political rivals attempted to move past their old differences. Jaego's diary would no doubt spark a broad conflict that would disrupt trade and destabilize the northwestern region of Akados for years to come.

The characters could reveal the truth. Or they could destroy the diary and keep Jaego's secret and the peace. The choice is up to them. However, if the characters destroy the diary, award them 1,000 additional experience points. Jaego's spirit visits them one last time and thanks them for their choice. He then moves on to a happier afterlife than was offered by Orcus or the forces of the Lightbringer.

Further Adventure

The characters may continue their exploration of the Underworld for as long as they wish, though their time may be limited due to a lack of proper provisions and the prescripts about eating in the land of the dead. If they return to the Styx, they may summon the boatman to take them back to the land of the living. When they step off the boat onto the shores of the Styx, they instead find themselves at the site of Jaego's grave. Their friendship with Jaego may eventually reach the ears of Mercier and Brodchek, meaning the characters may find themselves facing assassins and bounty hunters working on behalf of both nobles.

ACOLYTE OF ORCUS   CR 3

XP 800
Human cleric of Orcus 4
CE Medium humanoid (human)
Init +1; **Senses** Perception +4
AC 20, touch 11, flat-footed 19 (+7 armor, +1 Dex, +2 shield)
hp 22 (4d8+4)
Fort +4, **Ref** +2, **Will** +8
Speed 30 ft. (20 ft. in armor)
Melee mwk heavy mace +3 (1d8 - 1)
Special Attacks channel negative energy 5/day (DC 14, 2d6), death's kiss 7/day
Spell-Like Abilities (CL 4th; concentration +6)
  3/day—*touch of fatigue* (DC 14)
Cleric Spells Prepared (CL 4th; concentration +8)
  2nd—*lesser animate dead, boneshaker* (DC 18), *ghoul touch*[D] (DC 18), *unholy ice weapon*
  1st—*cure light wounds, doom*[D] (DC 17), *grasping corpse, shield of faith, unhallowed blows*
  0 (at will)—*create water, detect magic, light, read magic*
  D Domain spell; **Domains** Evil (Demon subdomain), Death (Undead subdomain)
Str 8, **Dex** 13, **Con** 10, **Int** 12, **Wis** 18, **Cha** 14
Base Atk +3; **CMB** +2; **CMD** 13
Feats Greater Spell Focus (necromancy), Spell Focus (necromancy), Mage's Tattoo
Skills Acrobatics -5 (-9 to jump), Knowledge (planes) +8, Knowledge (religion) +8, Sense Motive +11, Spellcraft +8
Languages Abyssal, Common
SQ fury of the abyss
Combat Gear *potion of cure light wounds (2), potion of cure moderate wounds;* **Other Gear** *+1 breastplate,* mwk heavy steel shield, mwk heavy mace, golden unholy symbol of Orcus, holy text (Orcus), spell component pouch, 38 gp
Special Abilities
Death's Kiss (2 rounds, 7/day) (Su) Melee touch attack makes target count as undead for positive / negative energy healing / harming
Fury of the Abyss (+2, 7/day) (Su) For 1 round -2 AC and gain bonus to melee attack / damage / CMB
Mage's Tattoo (Necromancy) Spells from chosen school gain +1 caster level.

ANTIPALADIN OF ORCUS   CR 3

XP 800
Human antipaladin (knight of the sepulcher) 4
CE Medium humanoid (human)
Init +1; **Senses** Perception -1
Aura cowardice (10 ft.)
AC 19, touch 11, flat-footed 18 (+8 armor, +1 Dex)
hp 30 (4d10+8)
Fort +9, **Ref** +6, **Will** +7
Immune disease
Speed 30 ft. (20 ft. in armor)
Melee mwk weighted spear +7 (1d8 + 3/×3)
Ranged composite longbow +5 (1d8 + 2/×3)
Special Attacks channel negative energy 3/day (DC 16, 2d6), smite good 2/day (+4 attack and AC, +4 damage)
Antipaladin Spell-Like Abilities (CL 4th; concentration +8)
  At will—*detect good*
Antipaladin (Knight of the Sepulcher) Spells Prepared (CL 1st; concentration +5)
  1st—*litany of weakness*
Str 14, **Dex** 12, **Con** 13, **Int** 10, **Wis** 8, **Cha** 18
Base Atk +4; **CMB** +6; **CMD** 17
Feats Demonic Style, Furious Focus, Power Attack
Skills Acrobatics -4 (-8 to jump), Intimidate +11, Knowledge (religion) +7, Spellcraft +7
Languages Common
SQ touch of corruption 6/day (2d6)
Other Gear *+1 banded mail,* arrows (20), composite longbow (+2 Str), mwk weighted spear, golden unholy symbol of Orcus, holy text (Orcus)

ADROCULUS THE SACRIFICER   CR 11

XP 12,800
Human cleric (divine paragon, undead lord) of Orcus 12
CE Medium humanoid (human)
Init +1; **Senses** Perception +6
AC 24, touch 12, flat-footed 23 (+8 armor, +1 deflection, +1 Dex, +4 shield)
hp 67 (12d8+13)
Fort +7, **Ref** +5, **Will** +14; +4 profane bonus vs. death and negative energy effects
Defensive Abilities death's embrace
Speed 30 ft. (20 ft. in armor)
Melee staff of dark flame +10/+5 (1d6 + 1 + 1d6 fire)
Special Attacks death's kiss 9/day, undeath variant channeling 6/day (DC 21, 6d6)
Spell-Like Abilities (CL 12th; concentration +15)
  3/day—*touch of fatigue* (DC 15)
  2/day—*command undead* (DC 17)
  1/day—*slay living* (DC 20)
Cleric (Divine Paragon, Undead Lord) Spells Prepared (CL 12th; concentration +18)
  6th—*create undead*[D], *flesh wall, harm* (DC 24), *wither limb* (DC 24)
  5th—*blood tentacles, boneshatter* (DC 23), *slay living*[D] (DC 23), *unhallow, unholy ice*
  4th—*blessing of fervor* (DC 20), *divine power, enervation*[D], *rigor mortis* (DC 20), *unholy blight* (DC 20)
  3rd—*animate dead*[D], *appearance of life* (DC 19), *bestow curse* (DC 21), *blindness / deafness* (DC 21), *prayer, unlife current* (DC 19)
  2nd—*lesser animate dead, boneshaker* (DC 20), *defending bone, ghoul hunger* (DC 20), *ghoul touch*[D] (DC 20), *necromantic burden* (DC 20), *unliving rage*
  1st—*bane* (DC 17), *bless, cause fear*[D] (DC 19), *divine favor, shield of faith, touch of bloodletting* (DC 19), *unhallowed blows*
  0 (at will)—*bleed* (DC 18), *detect magic, light, read magic*
  D Domain spell; **Domain** Death (Undead subdomain)
Str 10, **Dex** 13, **Con** 8, **Int** 12, **Wis** 22, **Cha** 16
Base Atk +9; **CMB** +9; **CMD** 21
Feats Aura Flare, Command Undead, Deific Obedience, Greater Spell Focus (necromancy), Improved Channel, Selective Channeling, Spell Focus (necromancy), Toughness, Undead Master, Mage's Tattoo
Skills Acrobatics -3 (-7 to jump), Knowledge (planes) +16, Knowledge (religion) +16, Sense Motive +21, Spellcraft +16
Languages Common, Necronomus
SQ corpse companion, devoted domain, divine brand, necromancer's secrets, unlife healer, empowered
Combat Gear *staff of dark flame;* **Other Gear** *+2 breastplate, +2 heavy steel shield, headband of mental prowess +2 (Wis, Cha), ring of protection +1,* golden unholy symbol of Orcus, holy text (Orcus), spell component pouch, onyx (7, worth 50 gp each)
Special Abilities
Obedience (Su) You gain a +4 profane bonus on all saving throws against death and negative energy effects.
Aura Flare (DC 19) Flare your alignment aura to fatigue or stagger those who oppose it.
Command Undead (DC 21) Standard action, 1 channel energy, undead in 30 ft. obey your commands as per *control undead* (Will neg).
Death's Embrace (Ex) Heal damage from channeled negative energy.
Death's Kiss (6 rounds, 9/day) (Su) Melee touch attack makes target count as undead for positive / negative energy healing / harming
Invoke Death (Sp) Once a day, cast *slay living* as a spell-like ability. Those slain rise as a juju zombie.
Unlife Healer, Empowered (Su) Any abilities that heal undead are enhanced with metamagic for free.
Mage's Tattoo (Necromancy) Spells from chosen school gain +1 caster level.

Bone Gate

CR 11

XP 12,800
N Gargantuan construct
Init +9; **Senses** darkvision 60 ft., low-light vision; **Perception** +2
AC 23, touch 11, flat-footed 18 (+5 Dex, +12 natural, -4 size)
hp 142 (15d10+60)
Fort +5, **Ref** +10, **Will** +7
DR 5/adamantine and bludgeoning; **Immune** construct traits,
   immunity to magic
Speed 0 ft.
Melee bite +17 (3d6 + 6), 2 slams +17 (4d6 + 6)
Space 20 ft.; **Reach** 20 ft.
Special Attacks bone prison
Spell-Like Abilities (CL 15th; concentration +12)
   At will—*gate*
Str 22, **Dex** 20, **Con** —, **Int** —, **Wis** 14, **Cha** 5
Base Atk +15; **CMB** +25; **CMD** 40 (44 vs. disarm, 44 vs. grapple)
Feats Improved Initiative[B]
Special Abilities
Bone Prison (Ex) As a standard action, the bone gate can throw some
   of its bones at a creature within 30 feet—it must make a ranged
   touch attack to hit. These bones magically duplicate and form a
   cage surrounding struck creatures. Each round, the cage makes a
   combat maneuver check to deal the golem's slam damage, using the
   golem's CMB. If the check fails, the target is still trapped but takes
   no damage. The target can escape the grapple normally or can break
   out of the bones by dealing 15 points of damage to the prison, which
   has the same AC, DR, and saves as the bone golem itself. Damage to
   the prison has no effect on the golem. The golem can only have one
   bone prison active at a time. If it wishes to create a second one, it (or
   some other creature) must first destroy the existing one.
Immunity to Magic (Ex) The bone gate is immune to any spell or spell-
   like ability that allows spell resistance. In addition, certain spells
   and abilities function differently against the creature, as noted
   below.
   Magical effects that heal living creatures *slow* a bone golem (as the
   slow spell) for 1d4 rounds (no save).
   A magical attack that deals negative energy damage breaks any *slow*
   effect on the gate and heals 1 point of damage for every 3 points of
   damage the attack would otherwise deal. If the healing would cause
   the gate to exceed its full normal hit points, it gains any excess as
   temporary hit points. The bone gate gets no saving throw against
   attacks that deal negative energy damage.
   A *raise dead*, *resurrection*, or *true resurrection* spell negates its DR
   and immunity to magic for 1 minute.

Cainor the Skin Stitcher

CR 5

XP 1,600
Ghoulish human wizard 5
CE Medium undead
Init +1; **Senses** darkvision 60 ft.; Perception +1
AC 14, touch 12, flat-footed 13 (+1 deflection, +1 Dex, +2 natural)
hp 50 (5d6+20)
Fort +4, **Ref** +2, **Will** +5
Immune undead traits
Speed 30 ft.
Melee bite +2 (1d6 plus paralysis and disease), 2 claws +2 (1d4 plus
   paralysis)
Special Attacks ghoul fever, hand of the apprentice (6/day), paralysis
   (1d4 + 1 rounds, elves are immune, DC 15)
Wizard Spells Prepared (CL 5th; concentration +8)
   3rd—*fireball* (DC 16), *lightning bolt* (DC 16)
   2nd—*masterwork transformation, resist energy, touch of bloodletting*
   (DC 15)
   1st—*crafter's fortune* (DC 14), *mage armor, shield, unlock flesh* (DC
   14)
   0 (at will)—*arcane mark, detect magic, ray of frost, read magic*
Str 10, **Dex** 12, **Con** —, **Int** 17, **Wis** 12, **Cha** 16
Base Atk +2; **CMB** +2; **CMD** 14
Feats Craft Construct, Craft Magic Arms & Armor, Craft Wand, Craft
   Wondrous Item, Haunt Scavenger, Scribe Scroll
Skills Appraise +11, Craft (leather) +13, Knowledge (arcana) +11,
   Knowledge (dungeoneering) +7, Knowledge (local) +11, Knowledge
   (nature) +7, Knowledge (planes) +7, Knowledge (religion) +7,
   Linguistics +7, Spellcraft +13
Languages Abyssal, Common, Draconic, Infernal, Necronomus
SQ arcane bond (ring of protection +1)
Other Gear *amulet of natural armor +1, ring of protection +1,* arcane
   family workbook, masterwork leather tool, masterwork spellcraft
   tool, spell component pouch, wizard spellbook
Special Abilities
Disease (DC 15) (Su) Ghoul Fever: Bite—injury; save Fort DC 15;
   onset 1 day; frequency 1/day; effect 1d3 Con and 1d3 Dex; cure 2
   consecutive saves. The save DC is Charisma-based.
Paralysis (1d4 + 1 rounds, elves are immune, DC 15) Attack renders
   victim unable to move or take actions (Fort neg.)

Ghoul Lord Amien

CR 11

XP 12,800
Human ghoul lord cleric of Orcus 10
CE Medium undead (humanoid, human)
Init +2; **Senses** darkvision 60 ft.; Perception +6
Aura desecration aura
AC 25, touch 12, flat-footed 23 (+7 armor, +2 Dex, +6 natural)
hp 160 (10d8+80)
Fort +13, **Ref** +5, **Will** +13
Defensive Abilities channel resistance +4, death's embrace; **DR** 10/
magic; **Immune** undead traits
Speed 30 ft. (20 ft. in armor)
Melee +2 heavy mace +13 / +8 (1d8 + 6), bite +6 (1d6 + 4 plus disease),
2 claws +6 (1d6 + 4) or
bite +11 (1d6+4 plus disease), 2 claws +11 (1d6+4)
Special Attacks channel negative energy 9/day (DC 21, 5d6), create
spawn, death's kiss 9/day, ghoul fever, paralysis (1d4 + 1 rounds, DC
16), scythe of evil (5 rounds, 1/day)
Spell-Like Abilities (CL 10th; concentration +16)
1/day—*darkness, fear* (DC 21)
Cleric Spells Prepared (CL 10th; concentration +16)
5th—*boneshatter* (DC 22), *slay living*[D] (DC 22), *unhallow, unholy
ice*
4th—*bestow planar infusion II, enervation*[D], *hunger for flesh* (DC
21), *rigor mortis* (DC 20), *unholy blight* (DC 20)
3rd—*animate dead*[D], *bestow curse* (DC 20), *blindness / deafness*
(DC 20), *horrifying visage* (DC 20), *unlife current* (DC 19)
2nd—*bone fists, boneshaker* (DC 19), *death knell* (DC 19), *defending
bone, desecrate, ghoul hunger* (DC 19), *ghoul touch*[D] (DC 19)
1st—*bestow planar infusion I, divine favor, doom*[D] (DC 18),
grasping corpse, murderous command (DC 17), *shield of faith, touch
of bloodletting* (DC 18)
0 (at will)—*bleed* (DC 17), *detect magic, enhanced diplomacy, read
magic*
D Domain spell; **Domains** Evil (Demon subdomain), Death (Undead
subdomain)
Str 18, **Dex** 14, **Con** —, **Int** 16, **Wis** 22, **Cha** 22
Base Atk +7; **CMB** +11; **CMD** 23
Feats Command Undead[B], Death Field (Move), Spell Focus
(necromancy), Thanatopic Spell, Threnodic Spell, Toughness,
Undead Master
Skills Acrobatics -1 (-5 to jump), Knowledge (arcana) +16, Knowledge
(history) +16, Knowledge (nobility) +16, Knowledge (planes) +16,
Knowledge (religion) +16, Spellcraft +16
Languages Abyssal, Common, Common, Infernal, Necronomus;
undead telepathy
SQ command undead, fury of the abyss, summon undead
Other Gear *+1 reliquary breastplate, +2 reliquary heavy mace*, 388 gp
Special Abilities
Command Undead (9/day) (Ex) Undead lords gain Command Undead
as the feat, even if they do not meet the prerequisites for it. The
undead lord may use this ability a number of times per day equal to
three plus its Charisma modifier (minimum 1). It may only command
undead of the same type as it.
Create Spawn (Su) A creature slain by an undead lord rises in 1d4
minutes as an undead creature of the same type as the undead lord.
Spawn are under control of the undead lord. This replaces any other
create spawn ability the base creature possesses.
Death Field (Move, 10 rounds/day) (Su) As a move action, you can
exude deadly energy from your body. While this death field is in
effect, small plants wither and recoil from you, allowing you to ignore
the effects of difficult terrain caused by plant life and ignore the
effects of spells like entangle that compel vegetation to grasp at you,
provided the spell's level is 3rd or lower (the death field cannot affect
more powerful plant magic).
Any swarm that enters your space takes 1d6 points of negative
energy damage; this damage is applied before you are affected by
any swarm attacks, so if the damage is enough to destroy the swarm,
it does not harm you.

At the end of your turn each round the death field is active, you
take 1 point of negative energy damage, and you cannot be healed
by positive energy effects while the death field is in place. Magic
items and spells that protect against negative energy damage do not
protect against this damage, but if you are undead or have negative
energy affinity (or a similar ability), the death field instead grants
fast healing 1 while it is in effect.
Disease (DC 16) (Su) Ghoul Fever: Bite—injury; save Fort DC 16;
onset 1 day; frequency 1/day; effect 1d3 Con and 1d3 Dex; cure 2
consecutive saves. The save DC is Charisma-based.
Paralysis (1d4 + 1 rounds, DC 16) Attacks paralyze foes.
Summon Undead (1/day) (Sp) Once per day, an undead lord can
summon a total number of HD worth of undead (of the same type as
the undead lord) equal to its HD x 1.5. Undead lords cannot summon
an undead creature that has more HD than it does.
Undead Telepathy (Su) Undead lords can communicate
telepathically with any other undead within 100 feet, including
mindless undead such as zombies and skeletons.

Hukeesh the Necromancer

CR 5

XP 1,600
Human agent of the grave 1/ undead master necromancer (undead) 5
CE Medium humanoid (human)
Init +1; **Senses** Perception +1
AC 13, touch 12, flat-footed 12 (+1 armor, +1 deflection, +1 Dex)
hp 29 (6 HD; 5d6+1d8+7)
Fort +3, **Ref** +3, **Will** +7
Speed 30 ft.
Melee +1 dagger +2 (1d4 / 19-20)
Special Attacks command undead (DC 16, 7/day)
Spell-Like Abilities (CL 6th; concentration +8)
3/day—*touch of fatigue* (DC 14)
Necromancer (Undead Master) Spells Prepared (CL 5th;
concentration +9)
3rd—*animate dead, undead anatomy I, vampiric touch*
2nd—*lesser animate dead, blindness/deafness* (DC 18), *boneshaker*
(DC 18), *command undead* (DC 18)
1st—*chill touch* (DC 17), *grasping corpse, mage armor, repair undead,
unlock flesh* (DC 17)
0 (at will)—*acid splash, detect magic, light, read magic*
Opposition Schools Enchantment, Illusion
Str 8, **Dex** 13, **Con** 10, **Int** 18, **Wis** 12, **Cha** 14
Base Atk +2; **CMB** +1; **CMD** 13
Feats Command Undead, Greater Spell Focus (necromancy), Improved
Channel, Spell Focus (necromancy), Undead Master, Mage's Tattoo
Skills Appraise +13, Diplomacy +2, Knowledge (arcana) +13,
Knowledge (dungeoneering) +8 (+10 on checks regarding undead
creatures, +6 on checks regarding living creatures), Knowledge
(engineering) +8, Knowledge (geography) +8, Knowledge (history) +8,
Knowledge (local) +8, Knowledge (nature) +8, Knowledge (nobility)
+8, Knowledge (planes) +13, Knowledge (religion) +13, Linguistics
+8, Spellcraft +13, Use Magic Device +11
Languages Abyssal, Celestial, Common, Draconic, Infernal,
Necronomus
SQ arcane bond (ring of protection +1), bolster, inspired necromancy,
lich's touch, necropolitan, reanimator, unholy fortitude
Other Gear mwk silken ceremonial armor, *+1 dagger, cloak of
resistance +1, ring of protection +1*, spell component pouch, wizard
spellbook, onyx (worth 50 gp) (3), 13 gp
Special Abilities
Bolster (+2, 2 rounds, 7/day) (Sp) As a standard action, touched undead
gains desecrate spell benefits for duration.
Command Undead (7/day, DC 16) Standard action, 1 channel energy,
undead in 30 ft. obey your commands as per control undead (Will
neg).

Inspired Necromancy (Ex) When determining the maximum number of Hit Dice of undead he can control with spells like *animate dead*, a character counts his agent of the grave levels twice. This ability does not factor into how many undead he can create with a single casting of a spell.

Lich's Touch (5/day) (Su) At 1st level, the agent of the grave becomes a conduit for negative energy and the chill powers of death, allowing him to make a melee touch attack dealing 1d6 points of damage from negative energy per level of the agent of the grave class he attains. This ability allows him to heal undead minions, and himself upon attaining the negative energy affinity ability at 4th level. He can use this ability a number of times per day equal to 3 + his Charisma bonus.

Necropolitan +2/-2 (Ex) +2 on Diplomacy and Knowledge checks vs. undead and -2 on checks vs. living creatures.

Unholy Fortitude (Su) At 1st level, the agent of the grave can tap into his conviction and bolster his health. Starting with the hit points he rolls for gaining his first agent of the grave level and every time he gains a level in any class thereafter, the character may choose to add either his Constitution bonus or his Charisma bonus to the number of new hit points he gains for that level.

Mage's Tattoo (Necromancy) Spells from chosen school gain +1 caster level.

KREAL THE BOOKBINDER   CR 8

XP 4,800
Drow wizard (scrollmaster) 9
NE Medium humanoid (elf)
Init +3; **Senses** darkvision 120 ft.; Perception +2
AC 15, touch 13, flat-footed 12 (+2 armor, +3 Dex)
hp 41 (9d6+9)
Fort +3, **Ref** +6, **Will** +6; +2 vs. enchantments
Immune sleep; **SR** 15
Weaknesses light blindness
Speed 30 ft.
Melee +1 elven leafblade +4 (1d4/18-20)
Special Attacks hand of the apprentice (6/day), metamagic mastery (1/day), scroll blade
Spell-Like Abilities (CL 9th; concentration +11)
    1/day—*dancing lights, darkness, faerie fire*
Wizard (Scrollmaster) Spells Prepared (CL 9th; concentration +12)
    5th—*runic overload*
    4th—*absorb rune I, symbol of slowing* (DC 17)
    3rd—*explosive runes, illusory script* (DC 16), *sepia snake sigil* (DC 16), *symbol of exsanguination* (DC 16)
    2nd—*fiery runes, obscured script, page-bound epiphany, rune of rule, symbol of mirroring* (DC 15)
    1st—*authenticating gaze, incendiary runes* (DC 14), *memorize page, rune trace, secluded grimoire*
    0 (at will)—*arcane mark, detect magic, mending, read magic*
Str 8, **Dex** 16, **Con** 10, **Int** 17, **Wis** 10, **Cha** 15
Base Atk +4; **CMB** +3; **CMD** 16
Feats Arcane Builder, Craft Wondrous Item, Grisly Ornament, Harvest Parts, Inscribe Rune, Monstrous Crafter, Scribe Scroll
Skills Craft (bookbinding) +17, Knowledge (arcana) +15, Knowledge (dungeoneering) +7, Knowledge (engineering) +7, Knowledge (geography) +7, Knowledge (history) +7, Knowledge (local) +7, Knowledge (nature) +7, Knowledge (nobility) +7, Knowledge (planes) +7, Knowledge (religion) +7, Linguistics +15, Perception +2, Spellcraft +15; **Racial Modifiers** +2 Perception
Languages Abyssal, Aquan, Auran, Celestial, Common, Draconic, Drow Sign Language, Elven, Ignan, Infernal, Necronomus, Sylvan, Terran, Undercommon
SQ poison use, scroll shield
Combat Gear *scroll of blank tentacle* (CL10), *scroll of mage armor* (CL 4), *scroll of shield* (CL 4); **Other Gear** *+1 silken ceremonial armor, +1 elven leafblade, blessed book, traveler's any-tool*, book lariat, scroll belt, scroll box, scroll case, 23 gp, 4 sp

Special Abilities

Scroll Blade (Su) A scrollmaster can wield any paper, parchment, or cloth scroll as if it were a melee weapon. In the hands of the wizard, the scroll acts as a short sword with an enhancement bonus equal to 1/2 the level of the highest-level wizard spell on the scroll; a scroll with only a cantrip or 1st-level spell on it counts as a masterwork short sword. The scrollmaster is proficient in this weapon, and feats and abilities that affect short swords (such as Weapon Focus) apply to this weapon. A scrollmaster cannot wield two scrollblades at the same time.

Activating this ability is a free action. A scroll blade only retains its abilities in the hands of the scrollmaster. The scroll blade has hardness 0 and hit points equal to the highest-level wizard spell on the scroll. Each successful hit by the scroll blade reduces its hit points by 1; this damage cannot be repaired, but does not affect casting from the scroll. When its hit points reach 0, the scroll is destroyed.

If a scroll contains a spell with a metamagic feat, this ability uses the original spell level of the spell (a *scroll of empowered fireball* counts as a 3rd-level spell).

At 3rd level, when using a 4th-level or higher wizard scroll as a scroll blade, the scrollmaster can choose to reduce its enhancement bonus by 1 (minimum +1 enhancement bonus) to treat it as a reach weapon. For example, he could use a *scroll of charm monster* (a 4th-level wizard spell) as either a *+2 short sword* or a *+1 short sword* with reach.

At 5th level, when using a 4th-level or higher wizard scroll as a scroll blade, the scrollmaster can choose to reduce its enhancement bonus (to a minimum of a +1 enhancement bonus) to give any of the following weapon properties: *defending, frost, icy burst, keen, ki focus, shock, shocking burst, speed*. Adding any of these properties consumes an amount of enhancement bonus equal to the property's cost (see Table 15–9: Melee Weapon Special Abilities in the *Core Rulebook*). The scrollmaster must know the prerequisite spell or spells to craft the weapon property in question (for example, he must know *haste* to be able to give his scroll blade the *speed* property). This ability replaces the wizard's arcane bond.

Scroll Shield (Su) A scrollmaster can wield any paper, parchment, or cloth scroll as if it were a light wooden shield. In the hands of the wizard, the scroll grants a +1 shield bonus with an enhancement bonus equal to 1/2 the level of the highest-level wizard spell on the scroll; a scroll with only a cantrip or 1st-level spell counts as a masterwork light shield sword. The scroll shield has no armor check penalty, arcane spell failure chance, or maximum Dexterity bonus. The scrollmaster is considered proficient in this shield. A scrollmaster can use a scrollblade in one hand and a scroll shield in the other hand.

Activating this ability is a free action. A scroll shield only retains its abilities in the hands of the scrollmaster. The scroll shield has hardness 0 and hit points equal to the highest-level wizard spell on the scroll. Each successful attack roll against the wizard reduces the scroll shield's hit points by 1; this damage cannot be repaired, but does not affect casting from the scroll. When its hit points reach 0, the scroll is destroyed.

At 5th level, when using a 3rd-level or higher wizard scroll as a scroll shield, the scrollmaster can choose to reduce its enhancement bonus (to a minimum of a +1 enhancement bonus) to give it any of the following shield properties: *ghost touch, light fortification, moderate fortification*. Adding any of these properties consumes an amount of bonus equal to the property's cost (see Table 15–5: Shield Special Abilities in the *Core Rulebook*). The scrollmaster must know the prerequisite spell or spells to craft the shield property in question (for example, he must know *limited wish* to be able to give his scroll shield the *fortification* property).

If a scroll contains a spell with a metamagic feat, this ability uses the original spell level of the spell (a *scroll of empowered fireball* counts as a 3rd-level spell).

Lysipus the Bone Cobbler

CR 5

XP 1,600
Ghoulish human unchained rogue 5
LE Medium undead
Init +3; **Senses** darkvision 60 ft.; Perception +9
AC 17, touch 13, flat-footed 14 (+3 armor, +3 Dex, +1 natural)
hp 60 (5d8+20)
Fort +5, **Ref** +8, **Will** +3
Defensive Abilities danger sense +1, evasion, uncanny dodge;
  Immune undead traits
Speed 30 ft.
Melee bite +6 (1d6 plus paralysis and disease), 2 claws +6 (1d4 + 3
  plus paralysis)
Special Attacks ghoul fever, paralysis (1d4 + 1 rounds, elves are
  immune, DC 15), sneak attack +3d6
Str 10, **Dex** 17, **Con** —, **Int** 12, **Wis** 12, **Cha** 16
Base Atk +3; **CMB** +3; **CMD** 16
Feats Blood Feast, Grisly Ornament, Harvest Parts, Prodigy, Weapon
  Finesse
Skills Appraise +9, Bluff +11, Craft (boneworking) +13, Diplomacy
  +11, Intimidate +11, Knowledge (local) +9, Perception +9, Profession
  (merchant) +13, Sense Motive +9, Use Magic Device +11
Languages Common, Necronomus
SQ debilitating injury: bewildered, debilitating injury: disoriented,
  debilitating injury: hampered, rogue talents (esoteric scholar, follow
  clues), trapfinding +2
Other Gear *+1 bone studded leather, cloak of resistance +1,*
  masterwork boneworking tool, masterwork merchant tool, scavenger
  beetle colony (10), snuffbox (bone), 82 gp, 5 sp
Special Abilities
Disease (DC 15) (Su) Ghoul Fever: Bite—injury; save Fort DC 15;
  onset 1 day; frequency 1/day; effect 1d3 Con and 1d3 Dex; cure 2
  consecutive saves. The save DC is Charisma-based.
Paralysis (1d4 + 1 rounds, elves are immune, DC 15) Attack renders
  victim unable to move or take actions (Fort neg.)

Professor Axeworm Armitage III

CR 9

XP 6,400
Venerable human ghost arcanist 8
LE Medium undead (augmented humanoid, human, incorporeal)
Init -2; **Senses** darkvision 60 ft.; Perception +10
AC 14, touch 14, flat-footed 14 (+6 deflection, -2 Dex)
hp 97 (8d6+49)
Fort +8, **Ref** +0, **Will** +8
Defensive Abilities channel resistance +4, incorporeal, rejuvenation;
  Immune undead traits
Speed fly 30 ft. (perfect)
Melee corrupting touch +2 (9d6)
Special Attacks arcane reservoir (4/11), arcanist exploits (flame
  arc, item crafting, potent magic, school understanding [undead]),
  consume spells, corrupting gaze (DC 20), malevolence (DC 20), turn
  undead (DC 16, 9/day)
Arcanist Spells Prepared (CL 8th; concentration +13)
  4th (3/day)—*animate dead*
  3rd (5/day)—*lesser animate dead, create soul gem* (DC 18)
  2nd (5/day)—*command undead* (DC 17), *defending bone, false life*
  1st (6/day)—*cause fear* (DC 16), *grasping corpse, identify, infernal
    healing, restore corpse*
  0 (at will)—*arcane mark, detect magic, disrupt undead, light, mage
    hand, open / close* (DC 15), *prestidigitation, read magic*
Str —, **Dex** 7, **Con** —, **Int** 20, **Wis** 15, **Cha** 22
Base Atk +4; **CMB** +2; **CMD** 18
Feats Craft Magic Arms & Armor, Craft Wand, Craft Wondrous Item,
  Forge Ring, Haunt Scavenger, Scribe Scroll, Turn Undead
Skills Fly +17, Knowledge (arcana) +16, Knowledge (dungeoneering)
  +16, Knowledge (engineering) +9, Knowledge (geography) +9,
  Knowledge (history) +9, Knowledge (local) +16, Knowledge (nature)
  +16, Knowledge (nobility) +9, Knowledge (planes) +16, Knowledge
  (religion) +16, Linguistics +9, Perception +10, Spellcraft +16, Stealth
  +6, Use Magic Device +11; **Racial Modifiers** +8 Perception, +8
  Stealth
Languages Abyssal, Celestial, Common, Draconic, Infernal,
  Necronomus, Undercommon
SQ bolster
Combat Gear *robe of bones*; **Other Gear** *brass chatterbox,
  mockingskull, sleeves of many garments,* arcanist spellbook, holy text
  (Orcus), platinum unholy symbol of Orcus, spell component pouch,
  20 days of life
Special Abilities
Arcane Reservoir +2 DC or CL (11/day) (Su) Pool of points fuel exploits
  or can expend to add +2 CL or DC while cast spell.
Bolster (+1, 1 round, 9/day) (Sp) As a standard action, touched undead
  gains *desecrate* spell benefits for duration.
Consume Spells (6/day) (Su) As a move action, expend a spell slot to
  add its spell levels to arcane reservoir.
Corrupting Gaze (DC 20) (Su) Gaze attack deals 2d10 HP + 1d4 CHA
  damage.
Corrupting Touch (DC 20) (Su) Touch does 9d6 damage from aging,
  ignoring most resistances (Fort half).
Flame Arc (4d6 + 6 fire damage, DC 20) (Su) Use 1 reservoir, deal fire
  dam in 30 ft line (Ref half).
Malevolence (DC 20) (Su) Magic Jar a creature on the material plane.
Rejuvenation (Su) Ghosts can return after a few days.
School Understanding (6 rounds) Use 1 reservoir as a swift action to
  treat school ability at full level & gain other ability for 6 rds.
Turn Undead (9/day, DC 16) Standard action, 1 channel energy,
  undead in 30 ft. flee as if panicked for 1 min. (Will neg)

Ramn Pujab
CR 9

XP 6,400
Human shadowcaster illusionist (shadow) 10
NE Medium humanoid (human)
Init +1; **Senses** darkvision 60 ft.; Perception +1
AC 11, touch 11, flat-footed 10 (+1 Dex)
hp 45 (10d6+10)
Fort +3, **Ref** +4, **Will** +8
Speed 30 ft.
Special Attacks binding darkness
Spell-Like Abilities (CL 10th; concentration +12)
 3/day—*ghost sound* (DC 13)
Illusionist (Shadowcaster) Spells Prepared (CL 10th; concentration +14)
 5th—*shadow evocation* (2, DC 20), *vampiric shadow shield*
 4th—*animate dead, horrific doubles, phantasmal killer* (DC 19), *shadow barbs* (DC 19), *shadow conjuration, shadow projection*
 3rd—*lesser animate dead, appearance of life* (DC 18), *displacement, gloomblind bolts* (DC 17), *phantasmal reminder* (DC 18)
 2nd—*blindness / deafness* (DC 16), *blur, command undead* (DC 16), *corpse lanterns, shadow anchor* (DC 17), *umbral weapon*
 1st—*mage armor, repair undead* (2), *shadow weapon* (DC 16), *shield, unlock flesh* (DC 15), *vanish* (DC 16)
 0 (at will)—*arcane mark, detect magic, disrupt undead, read magic*
Opposition Schools Evocation, Transmutation
Str 8, **Dex** 13, **Con** 10, **Int** 19, **Wis** 12, **Cha** 14
Base Atk +5; **CMB** +4; **CMD** 15
Feats Ghost Whisperer, Observant Illusion, Resilient Illusions, Scribe Scroll, Shadow Gambit, Spell Focus (illusion), Mage's Tattoo
Skills Appraise +17, Bluff +2 (+4 vs. undead or when speaking Necronomus), Diplomacy +2 (+4 vs. undead or when speaking Necronomus), Intimidate +2 (+4 vs. undead or when speaking Necronomus), Knowledge (arcana) +17, Knowledge (planes) +17, Knowledge (religion) +17, Profession (merchant) +14, Sense Motive +11 (+13 vs. undead or when speaking Necril), Spellcraft +17
Languages Abyssal, Celestial, Common, Draconic, Infernal, Necronomus, Shadowtongue
SQ extended illusions (5 rounds), shadow spell slots (shadow spell slot, shadow spell slot), shadow spells, shadow step, shadowy specialization
Combat Gear wand of infernal healing (49 charges); **Other Gear** rod of the wayang, spell component pouch, wizard spellbook
Special Abilities
Binding Darkness (3 rounds, 7/day) (Sp) Ranged Touch attack entangles target and grants them concealment.
Extended Illusions (+5 rds) (Su) Increase duration of illusion spells by 1/2 level (permanent at 20).
Observant Illusion (Su) Can project senses through 3rd+ level figment or shadow illusion. Swift or move to switch from body to spell.
Resilient Illusions Your illusions can substitute a CL check for their DC if it's higher.
Shadow Gambit You can tap into the Plane of Shadow to momentarily lend reality to one of your illusion (figment) spells.
Shadow Spells (Su) At 1st level, a shadowcaster uses his shadow to prepare additional spells. He must spend his entire period of spell preparation in dim illumination to use this ability. He may prepare a number of additional spell levels of spells equal to the level of the highest level spells he can prepare.
Shadow Step (60 5-ft inc/day) (Sp) Teleport 30 feet per day, in 5-foot increments.
Shadowy Specialization (Ex) Increase the percentage of damage caused by shadow spells and summoned creatures by +20% (max 100%)
Mage's Tattoo (Illusion) Spells from chosen school gain +1 caster level.

Rat, Barrow (Ghoulish)
CR 1

XP 400
N Tiny undead
Init +2; **Senses** darkvision 60 ft., low-light vision, scent; Perception +1
AC 16, touch 14, flat-footed 14 (+2 Dex, +2 natural, +2 size)
hp 2 (1d8-3)
Fort -3, **Ref** +2, **Will** +3
Defensive Abilities stone skin; **Immune** undead traits
Speed 15 ft., burrow 15 ft., climb 15 ft.
Melee bite +4 (1d3 - 2 plus paralysis and disease), 2 claws +4 (1d2 - 2 plus paralysis)
Space 2½ ft.; **Reach** 0 ft.
Special Attacks ghoul fever, paralysis (1d4 + 1 rounds, elves are immune, DC 7)
Str 6, **Dex** 15, **Con** —, **Int** 2, **Wis** 12, **Cha** 5
Base Atk +0; **CMB** +0; **CMD** 8
Feats Weapon Finesse
Skills Acrobatics +11 (+3 to jump), Climb +10, Stealth +14
SQ swarm
Special Abilities
Disease (DC 7) (Su) Ghoul Fever: Bite—injury; save Fort DC 7; onset 1 day; frequency 1/day; effect 1d3 Con and 1d3 Dex; cure 2 consecutive saves. The save DC is Charisma-based.
Paralysis (1d4 + 1 rounds, elves are immune, DC 7) Attack renders victim unable to move or take actions (Fort neg.)
Stone Skin (Su) Once per day, as a standard action, a barrow rat can toughen its skin to the hardness of stone. It gains damage reduction 10/- for 1 minute.
Swarm (Ex) Barrow rats crawl over each other in an attempt to swarm an opponent. Up to four barrow rats can occupy a single 5-foot space.

Shandar the Lich Queen
CR 12

XP 19,200
Human lich necromancer (undead) 11
CE Medium undead (augmented humanoid, human)
Init +1; **Senses** darkvision 60 ft., life sight (10 feet, 11 rounds/day); Perception +24
Aura fear (60 ft., DC 20)
AC 16, touch 11, flat-footed 15 (+1 Dex, +5 natural)
hp 132 (11d6+66)
Fort +8, **Ref** +4, **Will** +9
Defensive Abilities channel resistance +4, rejuvenation; **DR** 15/bludgeoning, 15/magic; **Immune** cold, electricity, undead traits
Speed 30 ft.
Melee touch +4 (1d8 + 5 negative energy plus paralyzing touch)
Special Attacks paralyzing touch (DC 20), turn undead (DC 20, 8/day)
Spell-Like Abilities (CL 11th; concentration +16)
   3/day—*touch of fatigue* (DC 17)
Necromancer Spells Prepared (CL 11th; concentration +16)
   6th—*circle of death* (DC 23), *create undead*
   5th—*cone of cold* (DC 20), *plane shift* (DC 20), *teleport*, *vampiric shadow shield*
   4th—*animate dead*, *boneshatter* (DC 21), *enervation*, *hunger for flesh* (DC 21), *scrying* (DC 19)
   3rd—*lesser animate dead*, *create soul gem* (2, DC 20), *fly*, *halt undead* (DC 20)
   2nd—*boneshaker* (DC 19), *command undead* (2, DC 19), *defending bone*, *ghoul hunger* (DC 19), *skinsend*
   1st—*cause fear* (DC 18), *chill touch* (DC 18), *grasping corpse*, *mage armor*, *repair undead*, *unlock flesh* (2, DC 18)
   0 (at will)—*arcane mark*, *detect magic*, *prestidigitation*, *read magic*
   Opposition Schools Illusion, Transmutation
Str 8, **Dex** 13, **Con** —, **Int** 20, **Wis** 14, **Cha** 21
Base Atk +5; **CMB** +4; **CMD** 15
Feats Craft Rod, Craft Wondrous Item, Greater Spell Focus (necromancy), Improved Familiar, Improved Plane Shift, Scribe Scroll, Skin Suit, Spell Focus (necromancy), Turn Undead, Undead Master, Mage's Tattoo
Skills Appraise +10, Fly +5, Intimidate +9, Knowledge (arcana) +19, Knowledge (dungeoneering) +9, Knowledge (engineering) +9, Knowledge (geography) +9, Knowledge (history) +9, Knowledge (local) +9, Knowledge (nature) +9, Knowledge (nobility) +9, Knowledge (planes) +19, Knowledge (religion) +19, Linguistics +19, Perception +24, Sense Motive +24, Spellcraft +19, Stealth +9; **Racial Modifiers** +8 Perception, +8 Sense Motive, +8 Stealth
Languages Abyssal, Aquan, Auran, Celestial, Common, Daemonic, Draconic, Dwarven, Elven, Gnome, Halfling, Ignan, Infernal, Necronomus, Sylvan, Terran, Undercommon
SQ arcane bond (Rawhide, cacodaemon), bolster
Combat Gear *thanatopic metamagic rod*; **Other Gear** *crystal ball with detect thoughts*, *headband of alluring charisma +4*, wizard spellbook, crystal lens (worth 500 gp)
Special Abilities
Bolster (+3, 5 rounds, 8/day) (Sp) As a standard action, touched undead gains desecrate spell benefits for duration.
Fear Aura (DC 20) Foes in 60 ft are frightened (below 5 HD) or shaken for 11 rounds (Will neg).
Improved Plane Shift Only 1 round to identify portal's destination & auto identify plane you arrive on.
Life Sight (10 feet, 11 rounds/day) (Su) Gain special blindsight which only sees living and undead.
Paralyzing Touch (1d8 + 5 negative energy damage, DC 20) Touched foe takes damage and permanent paralysis (Fort part). Seems dead unless examined.
Skin Suit (1/day) As full-round act, hide in false flesh during the day.
Turn Undead (8/day, DC 20) Standard action, 1 channel energy, undead in 30 ft. flee as if panicked for 1 min. (Will neg).
Mage's Tattoo (Necromancy) Spells from chosen school gain +1 caster level.

Shandar's Familiar, Rawhide
CR

XP –
Cacodaemon
NE Tiny outsider (daemon, evil, extraplanar)
Init +4; **Senses** darkvision 60 ft.; Perception +15
AC 22, touch 12, flat-footed 22 (+10 natural, +2 size)
hp 66 (3d10 + 3); fast healing 2
Fort +4, **Ref** +5, **Will** +8
Defensive Abilities improved evasion; **DR** 5/good or silver; **Immune** acid, death effects, disease, poison; **Resist** cold 10, electricity 10, fire 10; **SR** 16
Speed 5 ft., fly 50 ft. (perfect)
Melee bite +8 (1d4 + 1 plus disease)
Space 2½ ft.; **Reach** 0 ft.
Special Attacks deliver touch spells, disease, soul lock
Spell-Like Abilities (CL 6th; concentration +7)
   Constant—*detect good*, *detect magic*
   At will—*invisibility* (self only)
   3/day—*lesser confusion* (DC 12)
   1/week—*commune* (CL 12th, six questions)
Str 12, **Dex** 11, **Con** 13, **Int** 11, **Wis** 13, **Cha** 12
Base Atk +5; **CMB** +3; **CMD** 14
Feats Improved Initiative, Lightning Reflexes
Skills Acrobatics +0 (-12 to jump), Appraise +2, Bluff +7, Fly +18, Intimidate +2, Knowledge (planes) +14, Linguistics +11, Perception +15, Sense Motive +15, Spellcraft +11, Stealth +14, Use Magic Device +4
Languages Abyssal, Common, Infernal; speak with animal (same kind only), speak with master, telepathy 100 ft.
SQ change shape (octopus, venomous snake; polymorph), empathic link
Special Abilities
Change Shape (octopus, venomous snake) (Sp) You can change your form as per *polymorph*.
Disease (DC 16) (Su) Cacodaemonia: Bite—injury; save Fort DC 16; onset 1 day; frequency 1/day; effect 1d2 Wis; cure 2 consecutive saves. The save DC is Charisma-based.
Soul Lock (1/day, DC 16) (Su) Ingest the spirit of sentient creature and regurgitate it as a soul gem.

Sir Ulatuan

CR 8

XP 4,800
Human antipaladin (knight of the sepulcher) 9
CE Medium humanoid (human)
Init +1; **Senses** darkvision 60 ft.; Perception -1
Aura cowardice (10 ft.)
AC 24, touch 11, flat-footed 23 (+10 armor, +1 Dex, +3 shield)
hp 77 (9d10+27)
Fort +12, **Ref** +9, **Will** +10; +2 vs. mind-affecting and death
Defensive Abilities fortification 25%; **Immune** disease, poison
Speed 30 ft. (20 ft. in armor)
Melee +1 heavy mace +12 / +7 (1d8 + 3)
Ranged mwk composite longbow +11/+6 (1d8 + 2/×3)
Special Attacks channel negative energy 4/day (DC 18, 5d6), smite
   good 3/day (+4 attack and AC, +9 damage)
Antipaladin Spell-Like Abilities (CL 9th; concentration +13)
   At will—*detect good*
Antipaladin (Knight of the Sepulcher) Spells Prepared (CL 6th;
   concentration +10)
   2nd—*darkness, desecrate*
   1st—*inflict light wounds* (3, DC 15)
Str 15, **Dex** 13, **Con** 12, **Int** 10, **Wis** 8, **Cha** 18
Base Atk +9; **CMB** +11; **CMD** 22
Feats Bless Equipment, Bloody Assault, Command Undead, Demonic
   Style, Power Attack, Toughness
Skills Acrobatics -5 (-9 to jump), Intimidate +16, Knowledge (religion)
   +12, Sense Motive +11
Languages Common
SQ touch of corruption 8/day (4d6), touch of the crypt
Combat Gear *+1 arrow, +1 dwarf-bane arrow, +1 elf-bane arrow,
   +1 halfling-bane arrow, +1 human-bane arrow*; **Other Gear** *+1
   full plate, +1 heavy steel shield, +1 heavy mace*, arrows (20), mwk
   composite longbow (+2 Str), *brilliant flash unholy symbol, cloak of
   resistance +1*, 6 gp, 7 sp, 5 cp
Special Abilities
Aura of Cowardice -4 (10 ft.) (Su) Enemies in aura are not immune to
   fear and take -4 to saves vs. fear effects.
Bloody Assault (DC 15 for Heal) Take -5 to all attacks and maneuvers
   until your next turn to add 1d4 bleed damage (DC 15 for Heal) to all
   weapon melee attacks.
Command Undead (DC 18) Standard action, 1 channel energy, undead
   in 30 ft. obey your commands as per control undead (Will neg).
Demonic Style Charge actions give additional +1 atk & +2 dmg.
Detect Good (At will) (Sp) You can use detect good at will (as the spell).
Smite Good (3/day) (Su) +4 to hit, +9 to damage, +4 deflection bonus to
   AC when used.
Touch of the Crypt (Ex) +2 vs. mind-affecting & death, positive harms
   & negative heals, light fortification.

Appendix B: New Items

Armor of Undeath

Aura strong abjuration; **CL** 13th **Weight** 15 lbs.; **Price** 18,910 gp
This *+3 leather armor* is crafted from the flesh of humanoid beings and is as soft and supple as one's own skin. The armor offers a +2 profane bonus to saves versus necromantic spells and an additional +2 profane bonus to saves versus the abilities of undead creatures used against the wearer. The armor is decidedly evil in its very nature, however, and gives a −2 to penalty to Charisma-based reactions from those who recognize the leather's source for what it is.
Feats Craft Magical Arms and Armor, *hide from undead*; **Cost** 9,535 gp

Leaden Knot of the Underworld

Aura faint abjuration; **CL** 3rd; **Slot** neck; **Price** 1,000 gp; **Weight** —
Leaden knots are sacred amulets woven into the wrappings of mummies to protect their physical flesh as it is projected into the Underworld before crossing on to the proper afterlife. However, a leaden knot of the Underworld is an amulet fused with a mild protective magic that causes lesser undead such as skeletons, zombies, ghouls, and such lesser spirits to look upon an individual wearing such an amulet as simply another of the dead and to generally ignore them. This is not to say that the dead won't attack someone wearing such an amulet, especially if ordered to do so, however unintelligent undead are unlikely to attack a wearer unless provoked.

Leaden knots of the Underworld are typically given as gifts from otherworldly powers to clerics of death cults, necromancers, and other travelers of the Underworld to help them avoid unnecessary entanglements with hostile spirits. The amulet affords no other protections.
Feats Craft Wondrous Item, *hide from undead*; **Cost** 500 gp

Vials of Life (Minor Artifact)

These vials are tiny phylacteries that the dead use to store years of life siphoned from the living, or pieces of their eternal soul that they sacrifice for goods and services within the city. The vials each hold one year of life. The vials of life are priceless vessels. Drinking from one of the vessels cures the imbiber for 4d4 + 4 hit points and cures any current non-magical diseases and reduces the physical age of the drinker by 1 year. However, drinking one of the vials while in the Underworld may curse the imbiber to remain as a prisoner of the Underworld forever! Each vial of life beyond the first has its own risks to drinking it. Each consecutive vial requires a DC 15 Fortitude saving throw. If the saving throw fails, the character ages 10 years for each previous vial that has been drunk. If the number of vials exceeds the maximum age for the character's chosen race, he or she dies and rises the following day as a lich shade composed of dust and memory. The DC increases by +1 for every vial imbibed by one of the living beyond the second.
Destruction A vial of life is destroyed if it is exposed to sunlight.

Wraith Armor

Aura moderate conjuration; **CL** 9th **Weight** 15 lbs.; **Price** 10,910 gp
This *+2 leather armor* allows the user to assume the incorporeal form of a wraith for 10 rounds per day. While in wraith form, the character gains a touch attack that deals 1d8 points of negative energy damage and ignores armor worn by the wearer's foe.
Feats Craft Magical Arms and Armor, *plane shift*; **Cost** 5,535 gp

ADVENTURES
WORTH
WINNING